A Hazy Shade of Murder

by

Evadeen Brickwood

Episode 1

EVADEEN BRICKWOOD

"A Hazy Shade of Murder"

This book was first published in paperback by
Evadeen Brickwood on KDP Amazon

Paperback Copyright © 2020 by Evadeen Brickwood
E-Book Copyright © 2020 by Evadeen Brickwood

Find this book in digital format also at:
Kindle Store, Smashwords, Neobooks and Tolino

First edition 2020 by Evadeen Brickwood on KDP Amazon

Amazon ASIN: B08N5LDX12
Amazon ISBN: 9798562365408
NLSA ISBN: 9781049206165

Cover Design by Birgit Böttner
Image Source: Pixabay
Book Layout: Birgit Böttner
Marketing: Alphalogic International

Charlie Proudfoot would rather not get involved in solving murders, but her friend Lerato Gwala, a private detective from Johannesburg, believes that Charlie's talent of intuition will give her murder investigations the edge. So Charlie agrees to help Lerato with just this one case.

In this Episode:

Maribel Sharma from Zurich is in seventh heaven when Deepak Misra, an eligible bachelor from England, proposes marriage. It seems to be a match made in heaven. Then, during their honeymoon in Cape Town, Maribel finds out about her new husband's hidden passions and all hell breaks loose. The millionaire's son is no stranger to murder and used to getting his way. Will the two sleuths be able to prevent charming playboy Deepak from going too far this time?

Other Titles by Evadeen Brickwood

In the time travel youth series:

"Children of the Moon" ("Remember the Future 1")

in the German Edition:

"Kinder des Mondes" ("Erinnerung an die Zukunft 1")

"The Speaking Stone of Caradoc" ("Remember the Future 2")

"The Secret of the Bird God" ("Remember the Future 3")

Novels:

"A Half Moon Adventure" (An Adventure Mystery)

"Abenteuer Halbmond" (German Edition)

"Singing Lizards" (A Mystery-Adventure set in Africa)

"Singende Eidechsen" (German edition)

"The Rhino Whisperer" (A Crime Mystery)

"Der Nashorn Flüsterer" (German edition)

Special Thanks and Acknowledgements

Many thanks to my late husband Peter, who patiently brainstormed the idea of this series with me. Cobus Griesel for lending his technical know-how, Kim Hunter of Tango with Text and my many beta readers for their constructive editing and proofreading efforts.

For Peter

Chapter ONE

The young woman on the backseat of the mini-van writhed in agony and clutched her head with both hands. There had been no pain at first, but now she could feel a massive headache coming on. She watched dark red liquid dripping down her neckline.

The thick fluid stained the pretty powder-blue summer dress she had carefully chosen for the outing this morning. When she tried to turn her head, the woman felt how her glossy dark locks became stuck in her chandelier earrings.

She couldn't speak to tell her husband of three weeks that she needed help. He should call the police, scream or do something - anything - to save her. Only a gurgling sound escaped her lips as she saw how he was looking at her. Why did he smile?

This January morning had begun pleasantly enough. The weather was brilliant, and she was looking forward to the trip. Her man had organised a vehicle so they could visit the famous holiday spot of Cape Point on the southern-most tip of the continent. Tourists could even climb a working lighthouse, but she was a little afraid of heights. The newlyweds had taken a few day trips, since their arrival in South Africa almost a week ago. He'd spared no effort or expense: a sight-seeing tour around the city and an animal park with the most exotic-looking birds and monkeys and a vineyard. They had eaten out at fancy restaurants every night; usually on some terrace that overlooked the ocean. Glorious sunsets were free-of-charge.

They were spending their honeymoon in this blissful part of the world, and it couldn't be more perfect. According to the brochure at the hotel, Cape Agulhas was a drive up the coast from Cape Point.

From here, one could see the jagged line where the blue Atlantic and the brown Indian Ocean met. By the looks of it, this was a sight to behold; just a rather long drive. She'd googled pictures of 'the meeting of the oceans' on the Internet, but to visit such an extraordinary place would be the cherry on top for her.

So far, the wine farm in Stellenbosch had been her favourite outing. After a tour of the grounds and a wine tasting, they'd enjoyed a lunch picnic with a group of tourists in the dappled shade of cork oaks. They'd laughed so much with these complete strangers, and she'd admired the stark landscape from the corner of her eye.

The farmer kept a flock of geese. He preferred the chattering birds to poisonous sprays to keep vineyard pests in check... and there had been butterflies, so many butterflies among the wildflowers... the young woman didn't know how long it was taking her to think all of this. Maybe she was still asleep and dreaming.

But then, she could not have dreamed that their hired minivan had suddenly stopped on the edge of the winding road as they drove along the mountain towards the coast.

She remembered waking up and watching the unthinkable unfold. Now the young bride was lying on the backseat gasping for breath, watching her beautiful dress getting stained blood-red. But maybe… just maybe, it wasn't happening at all.

Her thoughts became a little fuzzy, and she wondered why her hubby was just sitting there, smiling at her. Shouldn't he be anxious or worried, seeing the state she was in? If this was real, why didn't he plead with the men or hold her in his arms? Anything but stare at her and smile.

Her head had rested against his shoulder and she'd been lulled into a light slumber, while the driver deftly negotiated the steep road. It was such a comfortable feeling - that she could relax, trusting in the driver's competence and her husband's affections. She'd believed that he would come to love her in time, despite his secret telephone conversations and his inability to… to….

Her mother continually assured her that they would grow together as a couple and that all it took was patience. She'd wanted to believe it so badly, wanted to believe that she was worrying about nothing.

The sudden halt had roused her from a pleasant dream. Lunch at the Two Oceans Restaurant, the famed 'meeting of the oceans', and spotting diving whales in the distance. She sat up and saw that they had stopped on the side of the mountain. Across the road from the sheltered parking space was a concrete slab that looked like a viewing platform. The driver mumbled something about needing to relieve himself and wandered off between the rocks.

She'd yawned and prepared to ask her husband if he wanted to take in the view, while they waited. Before she could utter a single word, two men jumped into the van. One of them was wearing a shirt with red stripes. The young woman let out one startled scream. She hadn't seen them approach from behind the rocks, but that's where they must have come from. Her thoughts raced. What was this all about? She reached for her man, seeking comfort, and noticed that he'd moved over to the other side of the seat.

A split second later, she looked down the dark barrel of a handgun. Frozen with shock, she stared at the gun, noting how dirty it was. Then a loud bang ripped through the air, hurting her ears, and there was sudden pressure on her neck. What? Why? She shrieked in despair. What was she supposed to do?

The young bride kept staring at the men in wide-eyed surprise, feeling woozy. Nobody demanded money or jewellery or had taken their cell phones. Nobody had said hands up! Wasn't this how an armed robbery went down? She'd been shot in the neck. Just like that; no words were spoken. The impact had thrown her back against the seat and her ears were ringing. It felt strange being shot.

She'd always imagined that there must be pain, but there was only pressure. What was she supposed to do now? Wasn't something supposed to happen? None of the men appeared agitated, which was odd. The shock wave from the loud bang subsided and there were expectant looks all around. Why wasn't her beloved screaming at them to leave his wife alone? What did they want?

Blood-red. Powder-blue... Her thoughts slipped from her grasp again and wandered.

She was a married woman now. All these years she'd waited for the right man to come along, but ever since the lavish three-day wedding ceremony in Chennai, there had been a jarring note between her and her new husband. The problem was that he wouldn't touch her - at all. Not even a proper kiss, apart from the occasional peck on the cheek or forehead. The bride longed to be touched, especially by the handsome husband she was getting to know.

Everything else was perfect. Almost too perfect.

At the age of 32, it had been high time that she got married. She knew what everybody was thinking, and the unspoken pressure from her family had become intolerable of late. Her mother had dropped hints all the time and eligible bachelors seemed to fall out of the sky at every turn. She'd liked none of them. That's why the young woman couldn't believe her luck when a catch like this eligible bachelor had asked her for her hand in marriage at a picnic in Hyde Park almost a year ago.

She didn't know that much about him, only that his family was immensely rich, but she'd immediately accepted with delight. It was a dream come true. Not only had the womenfolk, under the headship of her overjoyed mother-in-law-to-be, set out to organise the entire event in India, but they had also transported her relatives all the way from Zurich to Chennai to attend the event.

She'd grown up in Switzerland, but they also had relatives in Denmark and India - in Goa, mostly. The expense for this was likely small change for his father, who'd made a fortune with his construction company. The wedding celebrations must have cost him a pretty penny, but she had chosen not to contemplate such mundane matters as money during her honeymoon.

It was such great luck that they had accepted her into the bosom of their family and she did not want to risk their goodwill. This was it. She had fulfilled the expectations of her family and had hit the jackpot at the same time.

What more did she want?

The newly-wed woman would enjoy herself and be patient with her new husband. But wasn't the point of marriage great sex and later... children? Not that she'd ever had sex before. Not like most of her friends and even her older sister, because for all her independent nature and modern upbringing, the young woman was deeply conservative at heart.

The reason she hadn't married until the age of 32 was her desire to become educated and work before starting a family. Luckily, her parents had supported her all the way.

Okay, her headstrong personality also had something to do with it, and if she wanted children anytime soon, she couldn't ignore the ticking of her biological clock any longer. It had been ticking away merrily during her studies in Lausanne and, although she enjoyed her work, marriage had always been on the cards.

Seriously, how many good-looking, eligible Indian men of 35 existed in this world? Men, who didn't mind marrying an educated woman her age?

Now the newly-weds were on their honeymoon, and she would make the best of it. South Africa had been his first choice of a honeymoon destination, although the wife of a family acquaintance had been murdered in a city called Port Elizabeth during a robbery-gone-wrong three years ago. Everybody in their circle knew about it, and that's why she'd had reservations at first.

It's such a beautiful country, her man had said, and added that he felt quite safe there. South Africa had a reputation for rampant crime and it was not exactly known to be safe, but she had decided that if her husband-to-be felt safe there, then so would she. As an Indian bride, she was expected to dedicate herself to becoming a good and loyal wife and not to question her husband's every decision.

The young woman drifted back from her daydream into an ugly reality. The blood-red liquid was staining her elegant outfit and she still couldn't move, speak or make sense of what was happening to her.

"That's what you call being a good shot?" Her beloved shouted.

He was addressing the man who'd fired the gun at her what seemed like an eternity ago. Good shot, good shot... The words echoed in her mind. Why was he shouting? All that shouting made her headache even worse.

Up to this point, their honeymoon in South Africa had been any bride's dream, her husband's lack of interest in physical relations aside. Even after the stress of the wedding spectacle was lifting, and they could finally be alone, he drew away from her whenever she tried to touch as much as his arm.

Hugging or kissing was out of the question. It wasn't supposed to be that way. He'd vaguely explained a certain condition to her during their wedding night in Chennai and promised to seek help on their return. Outspoken as she was, the young woman had confronted him in Cape Town about his alleged problem - well downstairs - again.

Despite the flimsy reasons he provided, she had agreed to wait and to be a good wife, until… she'd overheard a phone conversation on their second day in Cape Town. She'd walked into the lounge of their honeymoon suite, ready to have dinner at some fancy restaurant. One stupid phone call had changed everything!

It's all a misunderstanding, he'd assured her uneasily, and her instincts had gone bananas. She didn't mean to eavesdrop, but now she couldn't unhear that awful one-sided conversation either:

'No darling, I haven't told her yet. We'll discuss it as soon as I'm back from South Africa. No, not much longer, only another week. We'll get through it. Yes, you know that I do. Yes, I can't wait to see you either.'

She'd seen the mischievous look on his face as he'd turned around and how it had changed to a horror-struck expression. The young bride stood by the glass door, unable to move, while he was outside on the balcony. Speechless, they had stared at each other, unable to put what they were thinking into words.

The cheerful mood she'd been in was all but wiped

away. The newly-wed woman had assumed that what she was dealing with was a case of impotence, but by the sound of it, it was nothing of the sort. She'd already begun googling cures for his condition to help him, and the last thing she'd expected was the possibility that he had a lover back home! They'd argued after that, and he'd clammed up. She told him that if this marriage was going to work, there would have to be open communication between the two of them and that he had no choice but to get rid of his mistress back home.

'Why did you ask me to marry you if you love somebody else?' She had asked him quite rightly; standing there, trembling.

'You don't understand. Yes, there was a lover, but we are just friends now. I don't know why I went through with it. This marriage. I thought I could change and become a good husband to you. I'm really trying.'

'That's not an answer. You did go through with the marriage. You have to explain to me what's going on. I'm your wife now.'

'I can't explain it. Not yet, anyway.' He'd stood there like a little boy caught with his hand in the cookie jar, but she would have none of it.

'What do you propose, we do now? Do you want to be married to me and have a lover on the side at the same time? Is that what you want? Tell me… where does this leave me?' She began to wave her finger at him.

'Please don't raise your voice at me. Somebody might hear.' He'd taken a step towards her, but she had stopped him with one quick gesture.

'That's what you are concerned about: that somebody might hear? You shame me, lie to me the entire time, and now I must be quiet?' She couldn't believe his arrogance! 'How can we be married if you lie to me?' The young bride was getting agitated and her hands were flying up and down like excited little birds.

'I… I don't know. I haven't thought it through… and I might love you in time… after a while at least.'

That was more or less where their argument had ended. Neither of them wanted to go out to dinner after that, and even a relaxing stroll along the Waterfront was out of the question. He wanted to think about the situation and had left the hotel shortly after. 'I'm going for a walk,' he'd said and came back late that night.

She had suppressed the urge to phone her family. Perhaps there is a chance that we can work things out, she thought despite her hot anger.

It was so confusing! Maybe he truly only needs time. She'd peeled herself out of her lovely new dress and done some thinking of her own while watching a soppy movie and eating chocolates.

Then her logical mind had kicked in. Was she prepared to live a lie, to stay married to someone who didn't love her and entertained a mistress right from the start? Her mother kept saying that first comes marriage and love comes later, much like a pot filled with cold water that starts boiling on a hot plate. But there wasn't even a hint of infatuation when her new husband looked at her. He was so cold and polite all the time. That could only mean that he was still in love with his mistress, right?

Perhaps leaving him wasn't such a bad idea, then. They didn't live in the Middle Ages anymore after all, and she could make her own choices as a modern woman. Their marriage could be annulled, but the dire consequences that awaited her stifled any plans of leaving her husband. They would make her responsible for his disinterest, despite her beauty and desirable body. Her to-die-for body, according to her cousin Ayla. That meant there would be no hope for a happy future that included children. The Indian community would regard her as blighted for life.

She had no choice... the young woman would have to make this marriage work somehow. After much deliberation, she'd fallen asleep. Exhausted from a blinding headache that was not much different to the headache that was getting worse now and made her head spin.

Her husband still looked at her with a cruel smirk on his face. What did it all mean? Was he trying to get rid of her so he could be with his lover back home? Nobody could be that cruel!

The man in the striped shirt who had shot her in the neck stood there without saying a word. She replayed the scene in her mind: he'd pointed the gun, and she'd stared at him in shock. A bang and then this red liquid that smelled a lot like blood, started running down her neck, soiling the front of her favourite summer dress.

"Give me that!" Her husband demanded and

ripped the weapon from the man. Then he pointed the gun at her. The red-striped gunman jumped off the van without his gun and her thoughts went round and round in her aching head. The pain she felt came from deep inside.

The driver now stood behind her man, holding onto the top of the front seat, gawking at her. Could he perhaps help? Was there a hint of compassion in his eyes? She raised her hand. The driver's name was Thutso… Thutso.

The driver named Thutso looked at her with a lot less smugness than her husband. He looked scared. She held out her hand, wordlessly asking for his help. But he just watched as her husband ripped the thin fleece throw from her lap, wrapped it around the weapon and took aim.

This man, her husband only in name, meant her harm! The young bride realised with a chilling start that nobody would help her. She also realised with a twinge of sadness that she would not survive her honeymoon and most certainly die a virgin.

*

The dogs were barking: wake up, wake up, wake up!

"Oh gosh, not again!" Charlie Proudfoot groaned as she sat up. The second shot woke her up every time. It was one of those awful nightmares that kept plaguing her of late. In her dream, she experienced a young woman's thoughts and memories and her anguish at her husband's deception.

None of this had anything to do with Charlie. It was just a dream, and she even knew it while she was dreaming. But she couldn't help feeling as if it was her in that wretched mini-van. The dream seemed so real and in the end, the young woman always died at the hands of her husband. It wasn't a great feeling to be murdered, that's for sure!

Charlie Proudfoot dreamed a lot. Sometimes she was stuck in somebody else's mind - or that's what it felt like. In this kind of dream, she could be an old beggar-woman, sitting at a bus stop in front of a bustling bazaar or a blonde Swedish girl, who was approached by a local politician and his wife about a three-some.

Honestly, what the hell was she supposed to do about that in a dream? It was usually a one-way street and neither the emaciated beggar nor the beautiful

Swedish woman seemed to be aware of Charlie's presence. At least, the blonde woman had walked out of the restaurant when she had willed her to do so.

Charlie had no idea why she was dreaming so much, but she had accepted the situation a long time ago. Only being shot was on a whole new level. I hate those damn dreams, she thought sleepily. Why would I dream about being murdered?

Dammit.

Wait, what time was it? Mercifully, the nightmare swiftly slipped back into the realm of dreams, and reality took hold again. The dogs were barking!

One last yawn, then she checked the wristwatch on her nightstand. It was 8:30 am. Oh, dear. She didn't have much to do these days and sadly, there was nobody to warm her bed to justify a sleep-in, but the dogs needed to be fed. Why were the dogs outside? Her brother Jono must have let them out then fallen asleep again.

It crossed her mind that the annoying new neighbours would take their large dogs to the park again like every morning around 9 o'clock. That was in half an hour. They had attacked Popcorn and Billie, her own two rescue dogs several times through the gate. Those dogs were not on a leash, and no one in the neighbourhood liked that very much, but the last thing Charlie needed was another confrontation. The old woman, who walked them, wasn't shy to break up a dogfight with the leash she should have put on her dogs. It was surreal. Charlie and Jono had decided that the woman must be senile because no normal person would do such a thing. Since then, Billie and Popcorn barked whenever they heard that woman as much as breathe.

Charlie didn't know the hag's name, but she must be somehow related to the couple and their three children. They spent a lot of time outside in the otherwise quiet street. The younger woman seemed to maintain a nail bar at the house. The smell of acetone sometimes wafted across the street and clients arrived and left at all hours. The husband went to work early in the morning and returned late at night in his very noisy, spluttering Mr. Bean car. Like… right now. That's probably why Billie and Popcorn were so upset. The car moved away and her dogs settled down.

The new neighbours had moved in after Charlie

and Jono, so strictly speaking, Charlie had seniority. Too bad they didn't care.

Jono had tried to speak to the husband – man to man – but nothing had changed. They simply called them The New Neighbours, the people on the other side where The Rich People and The Stewardess lived two houses down in the other direction. Charlie would meet all of them formally in time and learn their names, but she had no desire to make friends with someone who resorted to hitting her dogs!

Charlie threw the three duvets off, only to quickly cover up again when the cold hit.

"Argh!" She complained.

In Johannesburg, September meant early spring. It was better than autumn in New York, but South African houses were not built to keep out the cold. The season had begun to change rather late this year, and the temperatures were still freezing at night. Soon, it would be spring with trees and bushes flowering in every colour. Temperatures would soar and warm the house, but it wasn't spring quite yet. Charlie had been born here, but she didn't possess any recollection of her life in Africa before she was adopted by the Morake family. The memories of her childhood were firmly centred in New York.

Strange that in her dream it was always summer and the young woman was wearing a powder-blue summer dress. So it had to be summer wherever it was that she was being murdered.

Charlie resisted the temptation of letting herself fall back asleep and bravely hopped out of bed. Quick… the robe, socks and her slippers. In Johannesburg people had to deal with issues like the escalating price of electricity, making heating in winter a luxury for many. Such high electricity prices would surely have caused a riot in New York, but thankfully, the South African winter didn't last long - three months at most. And she had never heard of blizzards or frozen power lines, here.

I should get a gas heater, she thought and yawned again. Charlie trudged to the bathroom and studied her face in the mirror while brushing her teeth. She was pleased to see that the deep dark circles under her eyes were fading.

That's what grief could do to a person.

She'd inherited a cream skin tone, full lips and

long black eye-lashes from her Greek mother; her biological mother, that is. The auburn hair, facial shape and lean build had to come from her father's side. She couldn't be sure when it came to things like that. Her eyes were unusual because she had one blue eye and one hazel eye. A fairly rare condition called heterochromia iridium; quite a mouthful and few people noticed it.

She didn't know much about her father. Apparently, he was a Norwegian journalist who'd stayed in Johannesburg as a correspondent for a few years. All she had of him was an arty black-and-white photograph in a tattered envelope, together with colour pictures of her mother and grandparents and herself as a baby. An inconvenient baby.

In her early twenties, Charlie had wanted to know more. She'd found her father on the internet and printed the articles with photographs of him, folded the pages tightly and put them in a larger envelope. Both envelopes were securely stashed in her underwear drawer.

In the articles, he looked handsome and his eyes seemed so light… and he had a full head of auburn hair, greying a little at the temples. She'd never tried to contact the man who had given her life, but it gave her a sense of belonging. The Morake family, her true family, looked quite different from her. In fact, nobody in the Morake family looked alike.

How exactly her biological parents had met and fallen in love in the late eighties was still a mystery to Charlie, whose full name was Charlotte Dimitra Morake Proudfoot. Dimitra for her Greek mother and the surname Proudfoot came courtesy of her late husband Colin. Although a paternity test had proven that Sven Olson was indeed her father, her parents had never forged a family, because of Charlie's unplanned birth.

Her mother, Dimitra Papadopoulos, had somehow ended up running with the wrong crowd and when she died of an overdose in their tiny flat in Hillbrow at the age of twenty-two, her wealthy Greek grandparents had taken Charlie in for a short while. Then they'd decided that they were too old to look after an energetic toddler.

That's when her real parents, the incredible Morakes, had entered her life and fostered the spirited girl for a year. Her Greek grandmother had been against an adoption, but her grandfather died of a heart attack when Charlie was only four years old, and her grandmother no longer objected to an adoption. That's how she became part of the Morake family.

On the rare occasion her grandmother had come to visit, she would barely speak about her disgraced mother and her Norwegian father. The family in Norway didn't seem interested in her at all. It had bothered Charlie later as a teenager that Sven Olson had just disappeared from her life. Despite her adopted parents' love and support, she had struggled with this, until Colin Proudfoot began to surround Charlie with love and support. He was the only other person, who knew about the two envelopes.

Colin. Smart, kind, funny and good-looking. At first, Charlie had been reluctant to open her guarded heart, but after months of courting, the headstrong young woman had mellowed. Colin proposed five months into their relationship and one year later, they were married in a small ceremony.

She remembered being so very happy. They'd moved into a nice flat in New Haven, where Colin had his carpentry workshop and Charlie found a job as a technician in a laboratory. She was overqualified for the position, having studied genetics, but working part-time seemed like a good idea because they wanted a family.

Colin had been so happy when she'd showed him the test with the two blue lines. He had lifted her up and twirled her around. Colin's hands were so strong and sensitive at the same time. She could still feel his touch when she thought about this. Tears rose in her eyes. They didn't even know if the baby was a boy or a girl.

'I want a daughter,' he had said with a serious expression.

'But you will love our baby even if it's a boy!'

'Sure I will, but a daughter who looks like you would be a dream.'

'What if we're having twins?' She had asked him with a smile.

'No I don't think so,' he'd laughed. She could still hear his laughter that had warmed her to the core. Charlie wiped a tear from her eye and went into the kitchen to boil the kettle. No use wallowing in memories. The nightmare was all but forgotten by now.

She opened the kitchen gate and greeted the dogs outside in the driveway. Jono was probably in the cottage at the back of the garden. In his very own techno-space.

Billie snatched the first toy she saw on the ground for the usual tug of war with Popcorn. Billie ran excitedly into the kitchen and dropped the toy next to Charlie's feet. "You want me to throw that for you?" She asked the cute face with the large puppy eyes and Billie started wagging her tail.

"Alright then, here we go." She threw the toy down the length of the driveway and Billie zoomed off to fetch it.

Both dogs were from a rescue shelter north of the city. Billie was a beagle-cross and Popcorn a white poodle-thing. All the dogs at the shelter were crossbreeds and Charlie could have adopted every single one of them. Luckily, Jono had sense and told her he drew the line at two dogs.

Billie charged past her with the toy. She didn't have the bringing-back-part down just yet and preferred to chew the toy on the kitchen floor.

Charlie brewed herself a cup of Rooibos tea with vanilla flavour - her current favourite - and slowly drank the hot, milky liquid in the lounge. She had just tested her blood sugar and the result was promising. Her health had taken a nosedive after the accident eighteen months ago. The onset of diabetes could be an unwelcome side effect of the shock, the GP in New York had told her. He called it insulin resistance and with medicine and proper eating habits, the condition could be reversed. At first, Charlie didn't care. All she'd wanted was to be with the two people she loved most in this world, but her parents had insisted that she stick to the diet.

It had been an incredible shock - the accident on their way from New Haven to New York just before Christmas that year. If she had to describe how she'd felt during the weeks in hospital, it would be like being in an emotional coma.

Eighteen months ago, she couldn't have imagined surviving Colin and their unborn child for this long, but things had turned around after she'd decided to move back to South Africa.

The weird dreams of being in other people's minds had begun in New York and must have been triggered by the trauma as well. What else could it be? First, she thought she must have watched something on

Netflix but none of the movies had anything to do with Indian beggars or Swedish women. Instead, she'd binged on series about outer space and the cosmic phenomena they had so often discussed.

One of Colin's hobbies had been to watch the night sky through his telescope mounted on a tripod from the balcony of their second-story flat. She'd felt closer to him watching Netflix series about the hobby he had enjoyed.

Not that Charlie was a stranger to premonitions and dreams. She had always been a little on the intuitive side, especially as a teenager, but now she kept having those dreams about people she didn't even know in locations she didn't recognise.

She felt inexplicable guilt that she hadn't foreseen her own accident, hadn't been able to save her husband and child. Her intuition had let her down. But then again, Charlie knew that she wasn't psychic, so all this guilt was a useless emotion. There was nothing she could have done to save his life and the life that was just beginning to form in her womb.

At the funeral, everybody told her she had reason to be thankful that she'd made it through. But Charlie wasn't so sure about that. Seeing other mothers smile at their babies, pushing prams, was still painful to watch; not to speak of happy couples holding hands or sharing an ice cream cone on a park bench. It should have been her and Colin holding hands and their baby in a pram.

She had come to South Africa to make a new start, away from all the memories, and was grateful that her older brother Jono had come with her, but she couldn't help ruminating at times.

Colin, this blond hunk a bit on the pudgy side, had looked straight into her heart with his blue eyes. At least that's what it had felt like when they shook hands and he'd said that he could indeed repair the antique chest of drawers she had brought to him. It had been fate. She knew it sounded soppy, but Colin later admitted that he had seen the same in her eyes. These beautiful two-coloured eyes. Why could she still feel him, even smell him sometimes?

Enough of these thoughts, she decided firmly. It was time to find a job. Today. She had come to South Africa to move on from her grief, after all, and working was the best thing she could do.

Chapter TWO

There were exactly five companies in Johannesburg that advertised for somebody with her qualifications. She was over-qualified for three of the positions, but she would try to set up interviews, regardless. Charlie looked over the notes she'd made the day before when the phone on the chimney breast rang. Charlie lifted herself up from the carpeted floor.

'Oh hi, Dad! Having a late night again?' She loved her Dad dearly, loved it when he called her on the spur of the moment, just wanting to see how she was. 'It must be about three in the morning over there. I just got out of bed here in Joburg.'

She has banned me from the kitchen though, because of some birthday baking she's busy with for a neighbour's party tomorrow. Mom knows I have a sweet tooth. We're about to call it a night.'

'That's what I call good timing,' Itumeleng Morake chuckled. 'I'm still busy marking papers, darling, so I thought I might give you a quick call.

Can you believe that about a third of my students can't get their head around quantum mechanics? I wonder what Stephen Hawkins would have said to that. Your mother is also still up, keeping me company.

Itumeleng Morake was her adopted father and a tenured professor of Physics at the same university in New York, where her adopted mother, Motshabi Morake, lectured Management of Training. They were the best parents in the world.

Charlie had two brothers and one sister. The boys, Jono and Daniel, were adopted like herself. Jono was the oldest of the Morake-brood, then came Charlie and then Daniel. Her little sister's name was Leleti. She was the only biological child of the Morakes and their youngest. Mama Morake used to say that this family was her very own United Nations, and she probably still did. Charlie was half Greek, half Norwegian by birth, Jono was Korean and Mom and Dad had also adopted him in Johannesburg.

Daniel had joined them when they'd lived in Cape Town for a few years. He was coloured and better looking than Jono, if that was even possible.

Their youngest sibling, Leleti, had been born in

New York, so she was practically the only one who was not entirely South African. Leleti looked nothing like her tall and slender parents, although Dad kept assuring her that her stocky figure and darker complexion were family traits from his grandmother's side.

As the baby of the family, Leleti always had a sassy twinkle in her eyes and could wrap anyone around her little finger if she wanted to.

Jono's passion was computers; software in particular. Daniel was an aspiring lawyer and Leleti struggled through the last couple of years of high school.

'Stephen Hawking would have nothing good to say, I'm sure,' Charlie said and imagined her Dad sitting behind the large walnut desk in his study, marking papers or preparing lessons. As a little girl, she had come into his study and he'd let her sit on the big leather chair, watching him work. He would pick her up gently and carry into her room when she'd fallen asleep on the comfy leather chair by the window. Charlie had always felt safe with Dad.

'But I explained the basics to you when you were only twelve years old, mind you. You had no problem with the concept then. Why can't these students get their heads around it?' Charlie remembered lengthy conversations with Dad about space and time dilation, dark matter and the string theory.

'Dad, you can't always compare me to your university students. They can't all be struggling with quantum physics. Some of them must be geniuses. Plus, I grew up with you and I guess that makes all the difference.' She scolded him and drank some of her morning tea.

'And yet - you never walked in my footsteps. Microbiology and genetics were more your thing. Bloody waste of brainpower if you ask me.'

'Dad...'

'In any case,' Professor Morake said, 'I just wanted to see how you and Jono were doing. Is he behaving himself? I bet he's still asleep.'

Her brother Jono had given up a promising job in Silicon Valley and joined Charlie in South Africa when she told him, she'd sold her possession, the flat near her parents' home, bought a house in Blairgowrie and would leave New York in a fortnight. He could be quite spontaneous, her older brother.

'Jono is fine, Dad. He's helping me around the

house quite a bit and he even started to work as a technician on a freelance basis. It's keeping him busy. He let the dogs out earlier, but I haven't seen him, so I suppose he went back to sleep.'

'Well, he'll wake up soon enough, when your awful neighbour-lady walks past with her pack of wolves.' Even her family in New York knew about the terrible neighbours.

'Not everybody has friendly neighbours like you guys. I wouldn't throw this one here a birthday party, that's for sure,' Charlie countered.

'Your sister is going to a dance the day after tomorrow. Your mom is a bit nervous about it and gave her strict instructions to be at home by eleven.'

'Our baby girl is growing up. Leleti is not the type to run around with boys or stay out late. I wouldn't worry too much about it. Is she going with her friend Emma?'

'I think so, your mother knows about that.'

Popcorn and Billie started barking at the gate again.

'Speak of the devil... sorry Dad, I must get the dogs inside before the other neighbours jump down our throats for making a noise.'

'Right then, you better go. Speak to you soon, darling.'

'Bye, love you Dad.' They hung up.

Charlie ran down the length of the passage to the kitchen door that lead out to the driveway. Sure enough, the old woman ambled towards the park with her grandchildren.

"Popcorn, Billie! Come inside. Inside! Gamoto!" She often used the Greek swear word she vaguely remembered from her mother's frequent use of expletives when they had lived in the tiny flat in Hillbrow. Charlie didn't remember much of that time, just that she had been alone for long periods when she'd longed for her mother.

Charlie saw with surprise that the neighbour-lady on the other side of the road held the two large dogs on a tight leash. That's new, she thought.

Popcorn refused to listen and kept yapping. The big black dog had bitten him last week and there was no love lost between them.

Luckily, the wound didn't need stitches and had healed quickly. Finally, her two fur balls came running inside and sat down in front of Charlie, wagging their tails.

"I've spoilt you, haven't I?" She said to them and knew

that she shouldn't reward all that barking with treats.

Her brother had started this thing, giving them little treats during puppy training and now they expected them all the time. Billie with her cute Beagle-face and large sensitive eyes looked up at Charlie as if to say: come on lady, what are you waiting for? Popcorn, the aptly named white cross-breed sat down and waited patiently. Her brother Jono had been a great help with the dogs when Charlie had struggled with depression. Now she was taking control of her life again, bit by bit.

"Okay, I can't say no to such cute little faces," she said and rummaged through the treat basket on the shelf behind the door.

Her brother Jono appeared at the kitchen gate, pulling a beanie deeper into his face. "Who's barking so early in the morning?" He reprimanded the dogs. They answered him with wagging tails and happy yelps.

"It's not that early, bro," Charlie laughed. "Thanks for taking them out earlier."

"Anytime, sister. Is the old lady bugging them?"

Officially, Jono was her tenant, because it was too cumbersome to explain why an athletic Asian man with an American accent, who was her brother, was living with her. He stayed in the cottage at the back of the property, filled with computer parts and whiteboards. Jono was a nerd of note and Charlie liked a tidy house. They had barely unpacked the few things they'd brought with them when Jono showed her a new side to him.

He began to plant the garden. In the following months, he'd also paved a path around the house and built a shed with the help of Jetson, their once-a-week gardener. She'd kept the house interior simple with hardwood floors, thick carpets and wall hangings, but there was not a lot of furniture. They had painted the house and the cottage together and even constructed a fire pit with built-in seats by the back wall. Charlie was impressed. Who knew that her nerdy brother was a talented handyman?

The house and garden were fast becoming her sanctuary in the city.

The rest of the family had promised to come and visit. During the holidays, maybe. Life in New York kept them busy, but they spoke on the phone almost daily. I must get myself a mobile phone soon, Charlie thought. Jono couldn't believe how technically backwards she was. 'You can video-call them from your own phone', he had said. 'I'll come with you when you decide to buy one.'

The truth was, she kept forgetting small details like buying a cell phone, and would sometimes buy duplicates of grocery items they already had in the pantry. Grieving was mostly about forgetting, so the cell phone had to wait.

"Yeah," Charlie said while peeking out the kitchen window. "Somebody must have told her to put her hellhounds on a leash, but Popcorn doesn't trust them."

"Same old story. I think our pooches will hate them forever." He sighed and sat down on top of the kitchen table.

"Unfortunately... want some tea?"

"Tea? Nah, today I'll have myself a nice cup of coffee. Strong and black. I worked until the early hours of the morning on a software download. And thanks to our babies here, I didn't get my beauty sleep."

"Since when do you drink coffee?" Charlie filled the cordless kettle with water from the tap and switched it on.

"Since Rowena introduced me to it. Ethiopian coffee is apparently the best."

"I see… Ethiopian coffee… and this Rowena would be your new girlfriend?"

"I wouldn't call her that. We worked together on a job and she's the only woman I know, who can tell a DDR2 from a DDR4."

"Right, like I know what that means. So when do I get to meet this mystery woman?" Charlie winked at her brother.

"Maybe when she's back from Durban… we'll see."

It didn't sound as if he missed this Rowena much. "Okay then. By the way… Dad just called from New York. He wanted to see how we're doing all alone in crime-ridden Joburg."

"Can you blame him?" Jono scoffed. "Joburg has changed little in the past few years when it comes to crime. Endless labour strikes and electricity blackouts aren't helping. Why are you so tired, sis?" He got up and took two cups out of the top cupboard. "Remind me to paint the kitchen cupboards. You can choose the colour."

Charlie didn't seem to hear, so Jono would

patiently bring up the topic of painting the kitchen cupboards again at a later stage.

"Oh, I had that stupid nightmare again this morning. Overslept and now I must still feed the dogs. That's why there was a commotion at the gate. I didn't get the timing right, today." The water in the kettle bubbled and churned. Jono took the steaming kettle and made another cup of tea for Charlie and a Nescafé for himself.

"Pity we don't have the good Ethiopian stuff at home," Charlie teased him.

"Yeah, yeah." He added sweetener and milk to her tea. "Okay come, we can feed those naughty little buggers together before I go back to work."

Billie and Popcorn jumped up and down as if they understood what she had just said, then raced to the back where the dog food was kept in plastic bins under the veranda roof. Jono took the feeding bowls from the table with all the garden tools and Charlie carefully measured the pellets with a plastic cup. Billie did her usual little dance on her hind legs before the feed.

"Sit… sit… sit," Jono said slowly and both dogs

sat on their backsides and waited until he'd put their bowls on the ground.

"You've got them well-trained, I must say," Charlie praised. "What would I do without you, dearest brother." They chatted and drank their hot beverages, while the dogs wolfed down their breakfast.

"I wonder about that myself sometimes," Jono winked at her. "What did you dream about this time? I never dream like you. Only vaguely remember someone chasing me with their car and stuff like that."

"That's so sad." They laughed.

If she could tell anyone about her dreams, it was Jono. Her older brother would listen patiently and try to help unravel even her weirdest dreams without judging. Jono had always been on her side, even when they were kids. Especially in High School when Charlie was bullied mercilessly by a posse of girls in her grade.

They made fun of her unusual surname and that she had black parents. Being a free spirit, Charlie wanted to give them something to bleat about. She decided that 'Mermaid Blue' hair was the answer. Admittedly, she was only fifteen and hadn't thought her act of defiance through. First, she'd dyed her auburn hair a few shades lighter, which went virtually undetected, but when she'd tried out the striking 'Mermaid Blue', she'd gone a step too far.

She was sent home without much ado and the deed earned her a lecture from her adopted mom - who was a pro at lecturing - about setting an example as an older sister and that there were other ways to deal with bullying. Sure enough, Leleti and Daniel had giggled when they caught sight of the blue-haired Charlie and even Jono, who generally had her back, called her Arielle in a muffled voice.

Her mother had taken her rebellious daughter to the hairdresser before Dad could see her. Hearing the story without the visuals would be less upsetting. After that episode, things didn't exactly improve but having a handsome older brother had helped to spare her from further humiliation by the mean girls.

She hadn't been able to grasp that some of the girls at Edmund Hillary High in New York's West End, were simply jealous of her. Judging by the attention she received from boys, she wasn't bad looking, but Charlie knew nothing about being beautiful back then. Being pretty wasn't the only reason the popular girls didn't want her to sit at their table. She was sharp as a tack and unafraid to shake things up a bit. As a teenager, she'd hated her looks. She had felt uncomfortable in her own skin and tight clothes made her felt itchy and exposed. She preferred wide shirts and slacks, but she had to wear her school uniform like everybody else.

Jono had convinced her that if it riled the girls up that her hair had an unusual auburn colour, then that's the colour they would have to put up with.

"You should write your dreams down before you forget them," Charlie said. "I'd give you some of mine if I could."

"Thanks, sis," he laughed. "So what nightmare was it this time?"

"Oh, you know. I was again on the backseat of this fancy minibus with my… my husband. We were both Indian and on our honeymoon in Cape Town. The driver stopped on the way to Cape Point… to take a pee."

"Okay, I remember now." Jono took a sip of his coffee.

"Two guys jumped into the van and I was shot, but not dead. Then my dearest husband finishes the job himself, grinning like a Cheshire cat. There was blood running down my neck, soaking a light blue dress and caking my hair. I had really big earrings on. I was so sad and frightened."

Jono didn't bat an eyelash. "I see, it's the same old dream. I didn't know about the earrings, though. By the way, it's not Cape Point but Cape Agulhas where the two oceans meet and…"

"I know… we were going to that place afterwards. Are you even listening? My psycho of a husband had me killed, or rather, he killed me himself when I was not quite dead." Popcorn growled at Billie, who'd finished her food first and was busy sniffing around him curiously.

"Lovely, just that it wasn't you or your husband you were dreaming about," Jono reminded her. "It was somebody else's husband and we don't even know if these people exist. Maybe it's a symbolic dream."

"Yeah, you're right. It was not my husband – or even me. But it felt so real."

"You've always been a bit whack with hunches and dreams and so on, but a murder is a bit over the top." Jono finished his coffee. "Hey Popcorn, eat up."

Popcorn looked at him and munched the last few pellets in his bowl. "There you go." A bird landed on the back lawn and the dogs chased after it. Jono placed the bowls back on the table.

"I know it's weird. It must have something to do with Colin's death and the trauma of it all," Charlie said. "I felt not quite in touch with reality at the time. Like I wanted to follow him and got stuck halfway. At least that's how I felt."

"Yeah, I know. Sorry, sis." Jono gently wiped the tears away that were welling up in her eyes and she leaned against his shoulder. "That's something I can't fix for you. But it will get better. I promise. It might take a while but it will get better."

The dogs were running past them to check the front gate, only to come back immediately.

"Do you really think it will get better?" Charlie asked. She'd made his shoulder all wet again, but Jono didn't seem to mind.

"It has to. I've never had somebody die so close to me. Not that I can remember anyway. I mean as close as Colin was to you. That's bound to do some damage. But you are stronger than anyone else I know. Need a tissue, sis?"

He took a paper tissue out of his breast pocket and handed it to her

"Yes, thanks." Charlie dabbed her eyes with it. "You think I'm strong?" She asked in an unsure, almost child-like voice.

"A hundred per cent. Things will be alright, you'll see." Jono gave his sister a final bear hug before they walked back to the kitchen.

"Damn, I forgot to call the companies on my list!" Charlie said. Her eyes were still a little red.

"Still plenty of time for that. You can start right now." Jono deposited the cups in the sink. "Time for me to get back to work." He strolled toward the door.

"Are you going to cook for us tonight?" Charlie asked.

"Maybe…" Jono said. "Why, do you crave something special?"

"You know how much I love your green curry." She winked at him.

"Ah, I see. Alright then, why not?"

Jono Morake didn't mind indulging his sister. If that's what he could do to make her feel better, then that's what he would do. "Let's go shopping later. I just want to render this… thing… on my laptop."

"Thanks, I'll make my phone calls in the meantime. You are the bestest brother ever, you know," Charlie said and gave him a broad smile.

"Yes, I know." Jono took his beanie off and pushed his hand through his thick hair.

"You need a haircut," Charlie laughed.

"I guess I do. Okay, see you later, sis." He was barely out the door when the phone rang again.

"Hey, this place is like an office this morning," Charlie said and walked into the lounge. "Hello." She sat down on the carpet.

'Hello again, my dear,' Professor Morake answered.

'Oh, hi Dad, what's wrong?'

'Nothing's wrong. Well, first of all, your mother says hello. Your brother and sister are asleep, of course, or they would say hello too. Then there was something else I forgot…'

'What is it, Dad?' Charlie asked nervously.

'You do remember Lerato Gwala, don't you?'

'Lerato… yes, of course I remember her. We went to school together and I spoke to her briefly after Colin…'

'Yes, that one. Lerato phoned here yesterday, and I

forgot to tell you that she wanted your phone number in Joburg. So I gave it to her. I hope that's okay. She didn't even know that you'd moved back to South Africa. And she's also back in Joburg. Moved up from Cape Town. So maybe the two of you could get together and have a braai.'

It was obvious that her adopted father wanted her to socialise more and Itumeleng Morake loved a good barbecue as much as the next South African.

'Of course, it's okay. I haven't actually told anyone that I moved back, Dad. Did Lerato say what she wanted?' Charlie asked.

'Not really... at least not in detail. Only that it had something to do with her work and that she needed your help.'

'Okay, she can tell me herself what it's all about. I should probably get in touch with her in any case. A braai is a good idea or at least a coffee for starters. Thank you, Dad. Does she still work for the police?'

'She didn't say, but I assume so.'

'It must be getting late in New York. Bedtime for you, young man.' Charlie grinned. 'Give Mom a big hug from me and tell Leleti, she'd better listen to you guys about going out on a school night or I'll come over there – in person.'

Her Dad laughed his beautiful guttural laugh. 'Are you getting cheeky with your father? But I better not tell Leleti that. She will give us extra trouble if she thinks you're coming home to sort her out. Just to make you come.' She could virtually see him grin at the other end of the line. 'It's been a while since I pulled an all-nighter. Your mom's already in bed.'

'Just joking, Dad. I will phone you guys soon or Jono will. But we'll definitely phone, I promise.'

'Good, that's what I like to hear, Charlie. Must get back to working on those papers. Only three… no wait… four of them left to mark. Time to make myself a hot cup of coffee, now that I'm allowed in the kitchen again. Perhaps there is a cupcake waiting for me.'

'Don't work too long, Dad. I love you so much. Good night.'

'And a good day to you, my girl." Her Dad hung up just as Jono came into the room with the mail in his hand.

"Postman was here. What was that all about?" He asked and handed her some letters.

"It was Dad again."

"Why? Did something happen? Didn't he want to speak to me?"

"No, nothing happened. And he sends everybody's love. Also to you, in case you were wondering. Dad is still marking papers. He forgot to tell me that Lerato phoned and that she'd asked for my phone number in Joburg when she heard that I was here. You remember, Lerato Gwala, don't you?"

"Lerato? Sure I remember her. Even had a little crush on her in grade seven."

"No way! How come I didn't know about that?"

"Long time ago. What does she want, catching up?"

"Something to do with her work and that she needs my help," Charlie reported. "Lerato didn't even know that I was back in South Africa."

"That's odd... what kind of work is she doing again?"

"The last thing she told me was that she wanted to leave the police service and start a private detective agency with someone."

"She left the police force?"

"I don't know. It's tough to start your own business. I know that she worked as a detective in Cape Town. Now Dad says she's moved back to

Joburg. But I haven't spoken to her in a while. Not since... you know."

Jono knew. "Interesting. Maybe she wants you to get involved with the police. Detective Charlie Proudfoot. Has a ring to it. And getting out of the house isn't the worst thing, either. Better than working in a lab."

"Let's not get ahead of ourselves. I have no experience with police work. Maybe she wants me to help her go through some papers... something to do with genetics? Who knows?"

"Well, there's something she needs you to do for her and I think you know what that is. You've always been good friends, so she knows about your... gift. Speak to Lerato and find out."

"You know exactly that I'm not a psychic. There are people around who can do that sort of thing, but I'm certainly not one of them."

"Sure, no problem, sis. Have I ever called you a psychic? You can just do stuff because you are more sensitive than other people, that's all. You pay attention when others are sleep-walking through life. That's what I think."

"Does that include your sleepwalking?"

"Ha, nice one… but to an extent yeah, I guess. I'm not always wide-awake. Like this morning." Jono yawned as if on command.

"Drinking coffee and… you're still sleepwalking?"

"Just do me a favour and help Lerato with whatever it is she wants you to do. Forget about phoning those companies today. If it's nothing, you can still do that tomorrow."

"Okay, I'll think about it." Charlie opened one of the letters in her hand.

"Think about it? No, just do it."

"Hey, we don't even know what she wants me to do. Could be going undercover as a call girl."

"I'd do that, too."

Charlie chuckled. "That'll be the day!"

The phone rang again and this time Jono answered. 'Oh hi, Lerato. We were just talking about you. Yeah, tell me about it. Let me see if she's here… yup, she is and about to wrestle the phone from me. Hey, that hurt! She really needs to get herself a cell phone.' He handed Charlie the receiver and sat down to write a list of the ingredients he needed for his green curry.

'Hi Lerato, excuse my ill-behaved brother. My Dad just told me that you might phone.'

'Hey, doll. How are you doing? Are things getting a bit easier for you?'

'I have better and not-so-good days. Sorry I didn't let you know that I'm back.'

'It's not a problem. But I miss you, girl,' Lerato said.

'I just wish people wouldn't tell me what they would do if their spouse died all the time. It's like they are not even listening. But you always did.'

'Bummer, hunn. Don't worry about those pinheads. You let me know when you want to talk.' Charlie remembered how Lerato had been a loyal friend in primary school. She had even phoned her now and again in New York. 'Thank you. I guess things are slowly looking up again. Trying to find a job now.'

'Well, how about that...' her friend began. 'I have my hands full, starting the detective agency. You won't believe the hoops you have to jump through to get all the licenses and what not. Setting up a business, marketing and stuff like that,' Lerato sighed.

'So you did it? You no longer work for the police?'

'Not exactly. I work with the police now. I wouldn't get anywhere without our friends in the force. Andy and I started the Maitirelo PI agency.'

'Andy? Is he a boyfriend?'

'Andy Malherbe? No way, he's married. We were colleagues in Cape Town; well sort of. He worked more on the cyber-crime side, but he's got lots of contacts. And we are finally getting clients in. Small cases mostly. Cheating husbands and stuff like that. It's still tough. The law is one thing but reality is quite another.'

'You don't say,' Charlie quipped.

"What can I say? I'm passionate about justice and that's what we do. Justice. At least we are planning to do our bit. Andy is one of the good guys."

There was a pause.

'What do you need from me, Lerato? Dad said that it had something to do with your job. Do DNA tests?'

'What? No! It's a new case. A big one. I had a call from an overseas client two days ago … An Indian lady. Phoned me from England and it's something I would never have expected...' Lerato blustered.

'Yes, and?' Charlie interrupted her friend's torrent

of words. 'What about it?'

'In a nutshell? I need you, Charlie. I admit I'm not sure where to begin. Perhaps you could help me out for a while. As a consultant. I'll pay you…'

'Begin with what? Come on, shoot! Give me at least the gist of it.'

'You don't say that in our profession. Shoot might be taken literally,' Lerato scolded her.

'Even over the phone?'

'Even over the phone.' Her friend chortled, so it was possibly a joke.

"Come on, girl, spit it out. Do you want me to go undercover as a prostitute?"

'What?! No, of course not!' Lerato seemed genuinely shocked. 'What gives you that idea?'

'Jono suggested it.'

'Did he now? I'll get back to you on that some other time…'

'Then what do you want me to do?'

Charlie prodded her friend and moved the receiver to the other ear.

Lerato Gwala took a deep breath. 'It's more like crime prevention than an actual case. This client wants me to help her with a case that hasn't happened yet.'

'What's that supposed to mean – hasn't happened yet?' Charlie was confused and Jono stopped writing his shopping list to give her a funny look.

'Well, she's afraid that something might happen. A murder. I know… sounds crazy hey? But she's not as crazy as it sounds.'

'It sounds a little weird. What do you want me to do? Who is this client?'

'She's rich, but not crazy. Oh, wait, damn… there is a call coming in. Got to take that. I'll ring you back later…'

Click. Beep, beep, beep. Lerato had hung up, just as she was getting to the point.

Charlie grimaced and Jono grimaced back at her. They had a pretty good idea where this was going.

Chapter THREE

Nine Months Earlier

Maribel Sharma and her cousin Aruna hugged each other excitedly. As so often, they had been chatting on the bed in Maribel's spacious bedroom at the Zurich mansion when Maribel dropped a bombshell.

Aruna dribbled her feet in quick succession on the floor, hugging her cousin again. It was raining cats and dogs outside, but inside it felt as if the sun had just risen.

"Are you kidding me?" Her cousin yelled with delight. "When did that happen?" She grabbed Maribel's hand with the sparkling diamond engagement ring and admired it. "Look at that rock!"

"On Thursday in London," Maribel explained patiently.

"And you're only telling me now?" Aruna screeched with excitement.

"I'm still getting used to it myself." Maribel withdrew her hand. She pushed her hair back and shook her head. Now there wasn't much to push back, since the hairdresser had reduced her magnificent long mane to a neat shoulder length-bob. But it had become a habit, pushing her glossy dark tresses back all these years.

"You are getting married!"

Aruna was so thrilled that Maribel had to ask her cousin to lower her voice.

"Shhh. Maman is going to hear you and wonder what's going on upstairs." The young women usually called their mothers by the French term Maman, a habit that stemmed from their boarding school days in Lausanne. Aruna was a few years younger than Maribel, but they had shared some crucial years of their school life and shared many secrets during that time.

"And your parents are okay with the match?" Aruna said a trifle calmer.

"Why wouldn't they be? They are modern people. Goa is not exactly in the sticks and we've lived in Switzerland for as long as I can remember. Deepak is from a good family and that scores full points already.

His father owns some kind of company in Reading." She pulled her long slender legs up and leaned back against the large pillows. Her cousin copied Maribel's move.

"In Reading, I see." Aruna clucked her tongue.

"I'll have you know that Sanjay introduced us when I visited him in spring. So that's five months ago. If my brother knows him, he can't be so bad… and… he clearly respects women. Hasn't made a move on me all that time we've dated."

"Now that's old school! How does Sanjay know him?"

"Through university friends, I guess. I think that my parents put Sanjay up to it, setting me up with some of his friends. There were so many single, young men at that party he took me to in London. Can that be a coincidence?" Maribel shrugged her shoulders and smiled at the thought of her cunning family. Aruna's phone tinkled. She checked her Facebook posts and quickly liked a few comments.

"Your brother is a sly dog. And he never let on what he was planning to do?"

"I think he knew that I wouldn't like it if he set me up directly with someone. Like a blind date or something. I would have sent him packing for sure.

Last time it didn't go so well. He just asked me to dress nicely and put on more make-up. Men! But that's alright."

"Men are all the same. But your Deepak seems special."

"He is the kind and quiet type, you know."

"Aaah, still waters run deep." Aruna winked at her.

"What I mean is that he doesn't chase around after girls, although they'd hang around his neck every minute of the day if they could. He's so handsome. One or two of the girls at the party had their eye on him for sure."

"No wonder, with all that money in the family," Aruna said and typed a message on her phone at the same time. "He must be a real catch. I'm sure the Hindu mothers in Reading are on fire. Just waiting for a chance to introduce their roly-poly daughters to him. He's probably tired of all that attention by now. And you are playing hard to get? Men like that sort of thing."

"Oh, is that what I'm doing?" Maribel faked surprise.

"But he must have had at least one girlfriend or even a few. I mean, he's 35. Doesn't he tell you what he did with his life before you guys met?" Aruna pondered.

She had been in the loop about Maribel's boyfriend, but Maribel had been cagey about certain details.

"In truth, we haven't spoken about what we did before we met. Just normal stuff like studies and work. And I've met a few of his friends now. Sanjay told me that Deepak works for his father like half of the family."

"Hmm, I wonder what skeletons he has in his closet."

"Aruna! What skeletons are you talking about? Plenty of time to discuss things in detail when we are married, don't you think?"

"Shouldn't you ask him more questions about himself?" Maribel's cousin insisted. "Former girlfriends are an absolute must. What if you run into one of them and you have no idea who they are… and they exchange looks and what not and it becomes all embarrassing? Who knows, maybe he does have some skeletons in his closet… which makes him kind of interesting. Not that you have much to tell him," Aruna said and winked at Maribel again.

"Hey, slow down, Aruna. Your imagination is running away with you again! I'm not that boring!"

"What does he have to say about your boyfriends? I'm

sure your mother has sleepless nights about that issue."

"He doesn't seem to care much about my boyfriends or if I partied through the night. And… you know that nothing happened between me and Jean-Pierre."

"What does your fiancé do at his father's company?"

"What I know is that he's working in the accounting department. At least that's what Sanjay said. Although he seems to have the time to play cricket a lot and hang out with his friends."

"Rich boys don't have to go to work and he must have some muscles on him, then," Aruna screeched in a subdued sort of way, careful not to make too much of a noise. "Not bad. Like Sharukh Khan. He'll probably be alright in the downstairs department as well. You know… lucky you!"

"You can be so crude sometimes!" Maribel scolded her. "And he looks nothing like Sharukh Khan. More like Vikesh Siddarth."

They had gone to watch a historical movie with this Indian superstar a couple of weeks ago and both had fancied the leading man.

"Ah… that's too bad." Aruna feigned disappointment.

Maribel gave her cousin a reprimanding stare. "There is nothing wrong with Vikesh Siddarth, as far as I can tell."

"I'm just joking, Mari. Vikesh Siddarth is such a dish but I like Sharukh Khan better. Do you have a picture of this prince of a man?" Aruna demanded to know.

"No, I don't have a picture of him, but I can ask him to send me one on WhatsApp. He's good looking, just not like Sharukh Khan." She typed a message on her cell phone. "Wait… done!"

"Now it can only take hours for him to reply if he's that busy."

"He'll reply."

Anyone listening to their conversation would not have guessed that the two cousins were way past their teenage years. Maribel was pushing 32 and Aruna had just celebrated her 26th birthday, but they behaved more like teenagers when discussing boys or movie stars.

"So you talk on WhatsApp?" Aruna asked.

"Yes, of course, we talk on WhatsApp. We do communicate, you know." Maribel rolled her eyes at her cousin.

"So, he's rich and doesn't have to slog away like

some people to bring in the bacon. That much we know. Cricket is a gentleman's sport and you deserve a nice husband with time on his hands to make you happy, if you're getting my drift. Saving yourself for marriage all these years! He has nothing to complain about."

"Well, some of us still care about tradition. And that's not all there is to marriage anyway," Maribel gave her a knowing look.

"So prim and proper. You must talk. Choosing your husband all by yourself is not exactly traditional now, is it?"

"As long as my parents give their consent, I don't see anything wrong with it."

"What about his family? Wouldn't they like to see a younger woman pop out some offspring for them?"

"I'm not ancient yet. I can still have children. They know that I'm no spring chicken, of course, and they don't seem to object to his choice. People don't aim for five children these days. I'd like two. That's enough childbearing for me!"

"So what do your parents say?"

"They can't wait for me to become a married woman. We must still organise a meeting, but I think his parents are quite pleased with Deepak's choice of a bride."

"So when is the big day?" Aruna asked eagerly.

"We are still discussing that part, but I think his mother is aiming for late November. To be honest, I don't mind if she organises the wedding. I have so much on my plate at work," Maribel Sharma sighed. "I just hope that Maman will not be offended. The old Mrs. Misra can be a little bossy. They will have to sort things out between them." She shrugged her shoulders.

"You're not telling me that you want to work until the wedding?" Aruna clapped her hands in disbelief.

"And why not?" Maribel asked her.

A woman's voice called up the stairwell.

"Maribel, Aruna!"

"Yes, Maman? We're up here in my room," Maribel answered.

"Dinner is ready, you two! Wash your hands and come downstairs." The voice ordered them as if they were still schoolgirls.

"We'll be down in a minute, Maman!"

"Your Mom sounds cheerful!" Aruna noted gleefully. "Can't blame her."

"Well, her youngest daughter is getting married now as well, so she only has Sanjay to worry about. And from what I've seen in London, he's not exactly a shrinking violet," Maribel rolled her eyes and grinned. "I can tell you, the girls are mad about him." She beamed with pride.

"You don't say. If he wasn't my cousin, I wouldn't mind giving it a go."

"Don't you even say something like that!" Maribel clapped her playfully on the shoulder as they made their way to the door. "Haven't you heard about Sandra who married her second cousin on her father's side? I'm telling you, they won't have any more children; that's for sure."

"I'd never. You know me better than that." Aruna opened the door. The floors in the house were covered in cream wall-to-wall carpeting. Only Maribel had chosen a light pink colour for her room years ago.

The young women chatted away as they sauntered down the stairs. "I miss Darshini so much. Can you believe that it's already been three years since she got married in Copenhagen?" Darshini was Maribel's older sister, who didn't seem to have fertility issues. "They are trying for another child."

"No genetic problems there. Her husband is half Danish anyway."

"Although she's a doctor, Darshini says the goddess Parvati is looking out for her. You can't argue with that." Maribel sniffed the air. "Oh it smells delicious, doesn't it? I wonder what good old Rani has cooked for us tonight. When do you have to be back home?"

"I'll sleep over if it's alright with your parents. I don't feel like driving across town tonight. There is snow forecast and with all that rain, I'd rather not drive... hmm, it smells like curry."

"Yes, I'm sure it's curry. Mhmm, I love Rani's curries. Don't worry about staying here tonight. I'm sure Maman will be delighted to have you over again. Just let Auntie Aadiya know."

Aruna had whatsapped her mother before they'd reached the ground floor.

There was much to-ing and fro-ing between the kitchen and the dining room. Rani, the housekeeper, carried bowls with food into the elegant dining room and winked at the young women in greeting.

"Rani, put another plate on the table, please. My husband's business partner is joining us for dinner." Rani hurried to do what the Lady of the House asked of her without delay.

"Ah there you are, girls," Mrs. Sharma said. "Did Mari tell you the good news, Aruna?" She couldn't keep herself from beaming.

"She sure did, Auntie. Congratulations are in order! I'm so happy for her. For all of you!" The young woman clapped her hands exuberantly and gave her aunt a quick hug. The older woman gladly tolerated her niece's behaviour.

"Thank you, my dear. We barely have a year to plan the wedding. November in India. I've already told your mother and the rest of the family, of course. Oh, it will be the best wedding ever. Deepak's family is originally from Chennai, so we'll all go to India and then we'll have a civil ceremony in London and huge reception there as well. I can tell you, we need all hands on deck, even though Mrs. I'm told that Misra is taking over most of the preparations."

The cousins looked at each other and grimaced.

There would surely be sparks flying between the two matrons before the wedding day.

"So my mother already knows about the engagement?" Aruna asked.

"I just got off the phone with Aadiya." Mrs. Sharma said. "Maribel is so secretive. I want to shout the news of the roof and she wanted to tell you all by herself."

"Maman!"

"Whaaat?" Her mother asked on a long note. "You want to tell my niece but my sister-in-law is not supposed to know? That'll be the day. No, Aruna, you sit over here." She directed her niece to a chair opposite Maribel's.

"Oh, why?" Her daughter asked in surprise. Normally, the cousins sat next to each other. The rain drummed against the large window in the dining room and Mrs. Sharma drew the cream-coloured curtains.

"Papa is coming home any moment now with his new business partner. A nice young man from a good family. I haven't met him yet, but from what I hear, he's quite a catch. Good-looking, too!"

"Really, Maman? You are trying to set Aruna up

on a blind date with somebody you've never even met yourself?" Maribel exclaimed.

"Child, I would not call it that, but it can't do any harm to meet a nice young man of good breeding, now, can it? Aruna has not been as lucky as you - so far." The matron said and adjusted her hairdo in the large mirror above the sideboard.

"Give her a chance. She is a bit younger than me." The two young women laughed. "And we live in modern times."

Mrs. Sharma clucked and wiped an imaginary crumb off her yellow silk sari.

"Yes Auntie, I'm a modern young woman."

"Ah, nonsense! Modern women end up all alone."

Aruna sighed. Most Indian mothers were like that, but neither her mother nor her aunt knew that Aruna had begun to date a month ago. She truly liked a young man she had met at college.

His father was Indian and his mother was Swiss, which was not an ideal situation. There had been some drama before Darshini's choice of a husband was accepted into the family. So for the sake of peace, she had to play along in the eternal game of match-making. Of course, Maribel knew and pulled a face at her cousin.

"As long as he is good looking, I don't mind it so much. I just hope he's not too dull!"

"Ah, things were so much easier in my day. It can't harm if you have a little chat and see if you like him."

Mrs. Sharma hurried back into the kitchen. "Rani, the rain is getting worse. Close the curtains in the lounge, please."

Chapter FOUR

Lerato phoned back eventually. Jono had gone to the cottage to finish up his work and Charlie had already crossed out two of the companies on her list. They would go to the shops, soon.

'Sorry to let you wait, Charlie. That was a super-long phone call with some guy, who thinks his wife is cheating on him. I had to listen to every argument they've had. Andy is not in the office right now. His wife's having a baby soon - and all the calls come through to me.' She groaned. 'He's so much better at blowing people off.'

'You'll get the hang of it. What do you do if both of you have to go out?'

'We just moved into our office. The building management offers a virtual secretary service. Not cheap, so right now, calls are transferred to my cell phone. So what were we talking about before Mr. Jilted phoned? Oh yes, my new case...' Lerato focused again.

'Okay spill. What's going on with this case?' Charlie asked. 'Why do you need me to help you out? You said something about crime prevention? I have absolutely no clue when it comes to police work and all of that. I just worked in a forensics lab. We had quite a few samples to work with in New Haven, while I was there…'

Her friend interrupted her. 'We have labs here that do those tests for us. In this case, if anyone can help me, it's you.'

'Get off it! Why am I the only person, who can help you?'

'Because the crime hasn't happened yet and I need your help with that.' There was a pause. 'Charlie? Are you still there?' Lerato asked.

'Emm, yes, still here. Are you saying that your client is some sort of psychic or did she get an anonymous tip?' This conversation had taken an unexpected turn.

'No, not exactly an anonymous tip and she's not psychic either. At least as far as I know. This woman phones me two days ago and says that she needs our services. Got the agency's number from the internet and liked our rates. Also that I'm a woman detective. She lives in Zurich but was in London for a visit when she phoned. So here's the thing: her niece is getting married in India in November and the honeymoon is already booked. Some fancy boutique hotel in Cape Town. My client thinks that the new husband is planning to murder her niece.'

'What? So soon after the wedding? How does she know that?' This case sounded a little off.

'Apparently, she got hold of some e-mails and photographs. She says the groom is already planning the whole thing. Don't ask me how. And you should know what I need you for. How am I supposed to handle a case like that all on my own? I need more than e-mails and photographs. I thought you could feel the situation out. The honeymoon starts in two months and a bit, so we have to get cracking.'

'Wait a minute…we?' Charlie interrupted her flow of words, but Lerato would have none of it.

'Listen to me, please. I don't know anybody else, who's as intuitive as you are…'

'Intuitive? Good for you that you didn't say psychic.'

'Not a chance. I just remember how you knew

stuff at school before it even happened and I thought it might come in handy. Like when Audrey tried to play a prank on you and Nomsa and you didn't eat the bunny cakes and slapped the one cookie out of Nomsa's hand just as she was about to bite into it. Audrey got expelled for bringing drugs to school and I was suspended for a week… thanks for taking notes for me by the way…'

'Pleasure…' Of course, Charlie remembered.

'It was a stupid prank. But how did you even know that there was dagga in those cookies? And then when we wanted to go out to that nightclub and you said, we shouldn't go, because you had a bad feeling and then there was a fire? Then you have these dreams. The list goes on.'

'Have you never had a hunch? If you put your mind to it you'll also learn to go with your intuition. There is nothing mysterious about it and what I know about police work is what I watch on TV.'

'Well, I'll never be as good as a sangoma when it comes to that.'

'My intuition? I'm not a witchdoctor, girl!'

'No, you're not,' Lerato back-pedalled.

'Why doesn't your client go to the police with her e-mails and what not?'

'She thinks they won't take her seriously and the young man comes from an influential family.' Lerato sighed deeply.

'But you're the expert when it comes to these things.'

'What am I supposed to tell the police here? By the time they look into the matter and verify the documents, it'll be too late. Plus, normally we get unfaithful husbands or wives and that stuff. Normal things like trying to find out if an employee has stolen cash or families that are looking for a missing relative. We sometimes use external forensics auditors or a polygraph examiner to get to the truth. But you are the only one I know with intuition. Can't exactly wire this husband-to-be up and do a polygraph test if he hasn't committed a crime, yet.'

'And what about warning his bride?"

'Yeah, that will go down well. I can't give you my source, but your fiancé might try to kill you... besides, many brides-to-be are willing to overlook red flags. So you see, I really need your help to figure this one out.'

'Hmm. I would come in as a consultant?'

'Yes, of course, and we'll pay you for your time.' Lerato Gwala said reassuringly. Charlie glanced at the list of companies she was meant to phone for job interviews. The top two names were crossed out and Charlie had scribbled the word jerk next to one of them.

'How long have you been doing this kind of work, Lerato?'

'Almost six years if you count my stint with the police service, and one year as a private detective. Why?'

'Do you think this woman is legit? I mean, why would she contact you of all the available private detectives in Joburg? She couldn't find a more experienced detective agency in Cape Town? Just because she likes your rates and because you're a woman?'

'You think she's up to something? Thanks a lot, by the way.'

'Or perhaps she's a bit mad,' Charlie mused.

'Oh come on now... first, she's up to something and then she's mad.'

'I'm just playing devil's advocate for your benefit.'

'She didn't sound insane on the phone. Maybe she

shopped around and she liked what she saw. I think that our website is way better than those of my way more experienced colleagues. Andy put a lot of work into it.'

'Could be… but it's still a little odd, don't you think?'

'Sure, I know that. But then… she's paid my fee upfront for three months, plus monthly expenses on invoice without a twitch.'

'So that's what it is! You couldn't turn her down, because of the money.'

'Well, yeah! It's not that we don't need the money, and since I quoted her three times the usual fee, I can pay you a good fee and build our reputation in one go.'

'Three times the usual fee? Lerato…'

'What? I swear I heard her giggle when I quoted the rough estimate over the phone. Our Rand is dirt-cheap overseas and a rich Indian lady like her can definitely afford it. She said all she wants is for us to find out if this shady bridegroom is a real threat and do what we can to prevent a crime. Was I supposed to tell her that we can't do it?'

'And you didn't even wait for me to agree?'

'Call it a hunch,' Lerato said smugly.

'A hunch, hey? Lol.'

'Not like your hunches, of course. The client did some groundwork in Reading, where she was visiting her Indian family. That's also where the groom is from. The plan is that I'll take over here in South Africa and report back to her. She'll send me the e-mails I told you about, some incriminating photographs and what not.'

'Did you say Indian? Her surname wouldn't be Misra or Sharma by any chance?'

'Well yes, in fact, it is Aadiya Sharma. She said she's the sister of the bride's father. How could you know that?" Lerato Gwala sounded gobsmacked.

'You won't believe it if I tell you…'

'Try me, Charlie. If I'm not mistaken it has something to do with your intuition. Tell me I was wrong to ask for your help.'

'Okay… well, I've been having these dreams for a while… ever since Colin… you know… and recently I started dreaming about this newly-wed Indian couple. Long story, but in the end, she gets shot. Anyway… the names Misra and Sharma keep going through my head when I dream.'

'Do you still think, I phoned you by accident?' Lerato asked a little too smugly.

'Maybe you are the psychic here.'

'Who's talking about being psychic? You mean intuitive,' Lerato Gwala retorted. 'I'll probably just need you for the odd brainstorming session, where you allow your intuition free reign. That would already help me tremendously.'

'Okay... okay, I can live with that, I guess. Did you say you are going to pay me for my services?' Charlie asked and put her call list on a pile of other documents.

'Sure, you'd be a proper consultant. We fill in timesheets and I'll pay the money into your account.' Lerato confirmed.

'Alright then, I'll work for you as a consultant.'

'Thanks for not letting me down. When can we meet? To do some brainstorming, I mean. Do you feel like having breakfast somewhere this morning?'

'We can meet at Cresta. Oh, and by the way, I'm bringing my brother with me.' Charlie felt a little excited to be working again, even if the job was unusual.

'Which one?'

'Jono.'

'Of course, I should have known, since he answered the phone.'

'Yup, he's the only one who lives here at the moment and he's my wellness coach so to speak. We need to go to the shops anyway.'

Lerato Gwala couldn't wait to see her friend and get started on this new extraordinary case. Charlie already had a dream about it. How thrilling is that? She thought. 'How does Cuppa Coffee at Cresta sound? Let's say in about half an hour?'

'Great, we'll see you then. Don't be late!'

'Am I ever?' Lerato asked innocently.

'Hell, yes.' Charlie chuckled.

"Good choice, sis," Jono said when Charlie put her phone down. He'd walked into the lounge and was eavesdropping while he played with the dogs. "I'd like to go to Cuppa Coffee. Great, so I'm scoring a free breakfast for being your wellness coach?"

"Am I making a monumental mistake, Jono? I'm not detective material. I need your advice."

"You'd be silly not to take that chance. I mean how cool is it to work as a detective?"

"More like a consultant."

"Right, consultant then. If it doesn't work out, you can go back to testing people's DNA."

*

"So, what's this dream you were telling me about," Lerato slurped her cappuccino. "Unbelievable that you knew the name of that client from England and all."

She picked at her Seretse Khama breakfast, while Jono tucked into the full Bill Clinton, he had ordered. All breakfast items on the Cuppa Coffee menu bore the names of historical political figures.

"Dreams are sometimes like that." Charlie had barely touched the food in front of her. It was the first time that she was meeting one of her friends from high school since they'd moved to Johannesburg and she felt a little overwhelmed to move out of her comfort zone.

She was still not sure that her decision to work with Lerato on the case was the right one. What would happen if it was fate and there was nothing they could do to prevent the murder? That would be a horrible blow. Then again, how could she turn down her old friend?

Lerato was beautiful and smart and had the most

infectious laugh. As usual, she was dressed in sensible clothes: jeans, a red jersey and running shoes. It seemed like no time had passed at all and they were just having a stroll around the mall after school.

"Come on, tell me what you saw in your dream. Don't make me drag it out of you."

Charlie told her about the gruesome details of the dream that she remembered so clearly, and Lerato listened spellbound.

"Are you saying that one of these guys who jumped onto the van only wounded her and the husband finished the job?" Lerato put another forkful of scrambled eggs into her mouth and Charlie took a sip of her red cappuccino.

"He shot her again. This time in the head. You should have seen his eyes. They were so cold and empty, while he was looking at me… her." She put the cup down.

"That guy must be a psychopath or something. I mean who would do that to an innocent young woman he just got married to? Are there no other solutions if he doesn't love her?"

"Like not getting married in the first place," Jono

piped up. "Asshole. I'm glad I didn't have to see him do that."

"Yes, exactly. The worst thing was that I could feel what she was feeling and having to think her thoughts. Poor thing was so scared and confused."

"Apparently, this bridegroom of hers has quite a bit of moolah or at least his family does," Lerato said and tucked into the fried mushrooms. "I mean he can afford a big wedding in India and a honeymoon in South Africa. I need to research his background while I'm waiting. Perhaps I could get Florence to do that."

"Who is Florence?" Charlie asked.

"She's answering the phone for a few businesses in our office building, like a virtual office, but she'd like to earn more money she said."

"Sounds to me like this guy is an entitled brat." Jono finished his breakfast first and pushed the plate into the middle of the table.

"Listen, my friend," Lerato addressed Charlie. "You need to eat your breakfast before it gets all cold. Don't play around with blood sugar problems. If you want to work with me, you need to be strong and healthy."

"Alright, alright." Charlie laughed and began to pick at her Winston Churchill breakfast only to stop after the first bite. "Let me think for a moment. I need to get my head around this case of yours."

"Understandable. Dreaming about a murder scene with all the details of the people involved… and you could see who pulled the trigger… and it hasn't even happened yet. Cool. Think aloud, while you eat."

Charlie started eating again. "I didn't even know if it had already happened or not. The young woman wore a summer dress, which makes sense when they get married in November. That's summertime in South Africa."

"I'm getting goosebumps."

"Pretty useless information, isn't it? I can tell you what they were wearing and looked like but nothing much comes to mind that could help us. Maybe there's nothing we can do." Charlie couldn't help but feel defeated.

"No, not at all. I mean her aunt contacted ME, remember? That's more than just coincidence. She wants US to do something about it. If this guy really plans to kill his wife, we have at least an idea of what we can expect. And we'll at least have some proof apart from your dream."

"But the police will not take you seriously with this kind of information right now, will they? Did Mrs. Sharma send you the emails and photos?"

"Not yet, but leave that up to me, doll."

"She's paid you quite a bit of money in advance. That should be an incentive if she wants to give you a head start." Jono said. "Must love her niece a lot."

"I'll do something useful with that dosh and open a few doors for us."

"You aren't talking about bribes, are you?" Charlie asked.

"What bribes? No, I mean I'll speak to my old precinct buddies in Cape Town over a drink, maybe lunch. It's good manners to pay for it."

"Right. Wait a minute… It's early September. You want me to come to Cape Town with you for three months?"

"No silly, not for three months. When the newly-weds are in town, it won't be so airy-fairy. Mrs. Sharma will give us the exact dates. We can invite my buddies to lunch or something and discuss the facts.

That's not bribery, right?" Lerato winked at her friends. "In the meantime, we'll do as much research as we can and collect evidence."

"There is only so much you can do with emails and photographs."

"We'll research our suspect. I already found out that there is a connection with Port Elizabeth. A cold case worth following up on. We can go there for a few days and do some recon. Good old police work. Who knows, maybe we'll hit on something. The more we can find out about this Deepak Misra, the better."

"Good old police work is your department, Lerato. I know nothing about that."

"You'll learn as we go along. You've always been a quick study."

"Whatever we do, please promise me that we'll try everything we can to stop the murder from happening." Charlie sighed deeply.

"Of course, we will." Lerato smiled. "That's what we are getting paid for after all."

"With some luck, you can stop this new trend. That South Africa is great for murder-holidays," Jono chipped in. "There have been a few cases in the news." He was getting bored watching shoppers walk by.

"We'll do what we can," Lerato said modestly and took out her credit card. "This one's on me. Better get going, I have to do some work at the office. Can't leave Andy with all the reports and follow-ups. Andy is nervous about the baby."

"Sounds like you've had a few jobs already. When is the baby due?" Charlie asked and began to eat her breakfast.

"The business is only just starting to take off… and the baby is due in three weeks. But you know how it goes. Babies have their own schedules."

Charlie tried not to think about her personal stab at motherhood that had gone so wrong. "That breakfast is really good. I like crispy bacon," she said.

"Let's do this well prepared. As soon as I have all the information from England, I'll put together a rough time table for our project and then we can get cracking. First, we do some recon in Port Elizabeth after I'm done with Mr. Jilted." Lerato Gwala stood up and two men at a neighbouring table followed her fluid movements with adoring eyes. She ignored them and picked up her bag.

"Those two guys were totally checking you out back there," Charlie said as they walked towards the escalator.

"What's a girl to do? African men like round butts and I can't deny that my butt is round." She shrugged her shoulders.

Charlie laughed. "You are sexy, that's it. I wish I had a round butt like you."

"Nothing wrong with your figure or butt, Charlie. I wish I was as slim as you. Makes it easier to run, but we never want what our mommas gave us, do we?"

Jono stayed out of that kind of conversation. A conversation he had heard a hundred times before between girls. Any girls. No matter how beautiful they were, there was always something they were not happy with.

"As soon as I have the e-mails and pics, we'll book a flight to PE and start our research there. How do you feel about a little trip down to the South Coast?"

"A working holiday? Sure, I'd love to go to PE."

"Alright, then. I'll give you a call when I'm ready and we can make arrangements."

"Hey what about me? Don't I get a free holiday in

PE?" Jono smirked.

"I'll let you know when I need you, okay?" Lerato said and winked at him.

"Ah well, then I'll stay in freezing Joburg and babysit the dogs and the house, while you two live it up on the coast."

"Oh, don't be too sad," Charlie said. "You still have coffee shops in Joburg and Rowena's company, remember?"

"Not a lonesome minute for me. Just shout when you need a computer hack."

"Sure kiddo." Lerato walked over to the parking-ticket machine. "Time to get back to the office. I hope the baby holds out for another three weeks, but you never know."

"Bye Lerato, give my regards to Andy," Charlie hugged her friend.

"Alright, guys. I'll be in touch."

"Think about this carefully," Jono said when Lerato was out of earshot. "Getting involved in crime-fighting is no cakewalk."

"I asked you at home and you were all for it."

"I'm just worried. I don't want you to get caught

up in the middle of something dangerous. I know you want to help Lerato, but it's not your problem."

"But it is my problem. I can't ignore that I had that dream, so I'm already in the middle of it. I promise I'll be careful. Thank you for looking out for me, big brother. But I need something to do, to be useful again. This case seems to be falling into my lap and if there's just a small chance of saving a life, I'll have to give it a try. Wouldn't you do the same?"

"You asked for my advice and this is it. But I see your point, little sis. Let's go and buy the ingredients for the green curry, or am I off the hook tonight?"

"No way, I really want some comfort food and you are the best cook I know."

"Thanks for the flowers, sis. Always glad to be of service." Jono gave a slight bow. They walked into the shop and the laughter died in Charlie's eyes. She saw a young woman pushing a pram with a gurgling baby in the bakery section.

Charlie's heart contracted painfully. Would she ever be able to rid herself of this pain she'd been carrying around since the accident? That useless feeling of what could have been and would never be?

It was better to fight it. She was still alive. Charlie turned abruptly to her brother, who was inspecting vegetables.

"Look, Jono." she pointed to a row of cans and smiled. "The coconut milk is on special today."

Chapter FIVE

"I hate it, I hate it, I hate it!" The young man was dressed in nothing but his black briefs. He was a bit on the lean side, but rather attractive. He threw the folded newspaper he'd been reading across the room. It landed on the wooden floor with the front page face up. It showed the official engagement photo of Deepak Misra, 35, a local businessman and his bride-to-be Miss Maribel Sharma, 32, from Zurich. Both were facing each other, smiling broadly.

"Alec, please! Don't be in a strop again. We spoke about this," the other young man, who was lying on the bed, groaned. He was covered in a silk duvet, resting against the softly padded headboard. In this small London flat hidden from judging eyes, he could be himself. Nobody cared who he was or what he was doing here.

"That doesn't mean I must like it," the half-naked man exclaimed. Alec sulked and crossed his arms in front of his hairless chest.

"No, but you know that I don't have a choice in the matter. She's our ticket to freedom," The man in the bed said patiently. This was obviously not the first time the two of them had an argument over this issue. "She's desperate for a husband."

"According to you. Ticket to freedom my ass. Ball and chain is what I call it. We both know that you can always say no. You don't have to go through with it just because HE wants it."

"You are making this harder than it needs to be. After that dreaded wedding and the honeymoon, everything will be back to normal. This is normal." The young man on the bed pointed to his boyfriend then to his naked self. His nipples were sore and bleeding a little after their vigorous love-making and the skin on his back smarted. Just the way he liked it.

"And your wife is just going to play along; just like that? As if she's not expected to live with you in the big house and have your children."

"Hell's bells, Alec. After the wedding, nobody cares what happens. As long as I produce offspring, I can do as I please. As long as I'm married."

"I hate you!" Alec raged. He let himself fall onto a

padded chair and pouted.

"Don't be so difficult. We'll deal with it when we get to that point. She's a reasonable person… apart from being beautiful. I think she might just be understanding – and you, my friend, might actually like her."

He looked past his lover. The windows faced the backyard and a portion of Hampstead Heath. The sky was a solid grey colour, although the pink net curtains made it look less drab.

"Pah, I doubt I will like her. Unless she's open to a three-some now and again."

"Alec! There will be no three-somes. She's a classy, traditional lady. She'll be the mother of my children. And beautiful women don't do it for me, hunn, you know that. I'm not like you."

He flicked his hand in a contemptuous gesture.

"How are you planning to make babies with her, then? Put a sack over her head?"

"There's an idea."

"What am I supposed to do, Deepak? Just sit around at home like a good little boyfriend, while you are living it up with your bride, in South Africa of all places? You know how much I would love to holiday in Cape Town. It'll drive me out of my skull to see you getting married to a woman like a prince in India and then you'll live with her, mere kilometres away, in your parents' palace. And it's already all over the damn newspapers."

Alec studied himself in the large mirror above the headboard - his blond locks needed a haircut from Fabio. He jumped up and paced the room.

"Who cares what they write? It's only the local paper and that's the whole point of the exercise. Why else would my father organise this charade? Wouldn't be surprised if he sent the photo and article to the paper himself. I know that he's got connections in the press. Some of his clients are very conservative and that's why we have to be so careful. If anything gets out, I'm in even more trouble. Please understand that, love."

"So what! Maybe you should just stand up to your father for once and tell him where to get off." Alec stood by the windows and glowered, the net curtains between him and the unfriendly world outside.

"Yes, like that's going to happen anytime soon." Deepak pulled himself up and shook his head. "All I need from you is to understand the situation I'm in."

"Why can't you do that for me?" His boyfriend turned around with a scornful expression. "We don't live in the Middle Ages anymore, do we?"

"You don't know my father like I do, Alec. He won't stand for it and he's getting suspicious, so I can't drive him too far. That's why this marriage is the best thing that could happen to us." Deepak Misra scowled. "When I didn't bring home a girlfriend by the time I was sixteen, he organised a visit to a brothel in London. Nice and anonymous, so there wouldn't be any talk. Wouldn't be surprised if he pays those slappers a visit himself now and again. Big boobs and arses... that's what turns him on. Yuck. Can you imagine?"

"Actually, I can. Remember that I worked in a brothel until about a year ago. And what I did there?" Deepak's lover made provocative movements.

"How could I forget? I'm paying you enough to stay out of those circles, aren't I?"

"Look. I don't want to seem ungrateful or anything, but you know how I feel about you. And it's just not right." Alec's face puckered up.

"NO, it isn't, but I'm doing the best I can. I should leave pretty soon before it gets too late. Just in case I'm being followed."

"Bloody hell. You don't think your dad would go that far?" Alec gawped at him.

"You never know. Better safe than sorry." Deepak started to get up and put on his clothes that lay on the floor.

"In two days at the Baron and Maiden? To liven things up a bit?" Alec grinned.

"I've already booked a room upstairs."

"Deepak, you dirty scoundrel. You read my mind. Just the way I like you taking care of me. Come here, I'm getting all horny again, hearing you talk like that."

The sulk on his face disappeared as Alec took the whip he had used earlier on his lover and slapped him gently across the buttocks with it, then a bit harder. He knew that Deepak couldn't resist the playful game they played so often. He would discuss the small matter of an advance for next month's upkeep. Afterwards.

*

The elderly man, dressed as befitted a gentleman in modern-day London, stood outside the flat building in Crissenden Park and looked up. It was a good area and certainly not the cheapest. He had been waiting for an hour now, give or take. The private detective had given him this address and the time his son would be upstairs in this unassuming flat building.

His limousine driver had parked the car around the corner, so as not to arouse suspicion. When he decided to walk the distance to the entrance, it had begun to drizzle. Ashwin Misra moved under the canopy of a tree and opened his charcoal-coloured umbrella. He had come all the way from Reading to see it with his own eyes.

He would confront his son if the information proved correct. Mr. Misra had cancelled all his meetings this afternoon. Not that he had much time to spare. His thriving construction business didn't run itself. He was becoming impatient as if Deepak was making him wait on purpose. He could think of a thousand things he'd rather do than stand around in the drizzling rain and wait for his son, but the family's honour was at stake. So Ashwin Misra waited.

He had taught his children that 'with great wealth

comes great responsibility'. One's family's reputation was most important. What more could a father do? Deepak never seemed to understand the word responsibility. It was all his wife's fault. Mrs. Misra had mollycoddled her three sons from the time they'd left the womb. So, no wonder that they needed some discipline now and again. Maybe he should have been harsher on them and given them more frequent hidings, but what did it help to cry over spilled milk.

His two older sons did honour to the family name, but Deepak had always been a playboy at heart. And now this! At first, he'd not believed the private detective he had hired when his son couldn't explain his frequent absences or why playing cricket was more important than concluding a deal with the Italians.

Then he'd seen the photographs. He had been angry at first. Very angry. What was the use of that? He needed to reign in his youngest son and with some luck, it would not be too late. Deepak needed to understand that his playboy life was over, that he had responsibilities toward the family.

Just where was Deepak? He looked at his golden Rolex watch and put more weight on his left foot. The

PI had informed him that his son usually left the flat of his friend around this time and took the bus, then the tube to another destination with a broad grin on his face. That destination was a certain guest house in central London, where you could hire a room for a few quid an hour and was frequented by not so lady-like women.

Mr. Misra was here to find out what his son was up to when he said he was visiting clients and friends in London. Well, he already had found out more than he could stomach. Now that Deepak was engaged to a lovely, suitable woman, he had hoped that such tendencies would stop - at least for a while. Just where should one draw the line?

The front door opened and Ashwin Misra steeled himself, holding his umbrella up a little higher. He had to be firm and not give in to Deepak's charming smile and puppy eyes this time. Enough was enough.

Deepak Misra stepped out into the open and surveyed the grey sky above the foliage of the sycamore trees. He shielded his eyes with his hand against the drizzle. Uggh, rain again, he thought and opened his umbrella. Then he caught sight of his father and grew pale. For a second he had the crazy idea that fleeing down the street would save him from the scrutiny of his old man. Instead of running away, he had no choice but to confront his father.

"So, Deepak," he said sternly. "I've heard your conduct hasn't changed one bit since your engagement. Yes, I know everything about your little friend upstairs. And I don't want to know what exactly is going on between the two of you, but this has to stop. Right now. You are an engaged man now, and your future wife will not like such conduct. Family comes first."

Ashwin Misra stopped speaking and took a deep breath. He was not used to long speeches unless they had something to do with business.

The sun made a brief appearance between swirling grey clouds. He watched a woman, who hastened past, pulling a suitcase on castors up and down the kerb. He turned his attention back to his son, who stared at the wet ground under his colourful umbrella, like a little boy who was given a talking-to. He could not be at all sure that Deepak had listened to what he'd said.

"Let's take a walk in the park," he suggested. "Hampstead Heath is just up the road. I can give you half an hour."

"Yes, father," his son whispered.

They started walking in silence and the limousine followed them at a snail's pace to the nearby park. Deepak trotted along the path next to his father, who threatened to cut him off from his trust fund if he didn't change his ways. He'd heard all of this before in a million different variations and all he could think about was the next lover who was waiting for him at the cheap hotel in town for a wonderfully sordid experience. She wouldn't be please if he was late for their rendezvous.

Ashwin Misra's last-ditch attempt to turn around his son's ways, made Deepak only sneer on the inside. Outwardly, he was demure and listened obediently. He hated to be out in the rain and wanted to end this wigging as quickly as possible. How had his father found out again? This was his day and he wanted to spend it in his very own fashion. These sleazy encounters helped him face life in Reading again, to play his role in the next act of family life. To help him cope with the engagement to Maribel Sharma, and everything else that life was throwing at him without mercy. Now he had to change his routine!

"Thank you father, I promise I will mend my ways," Deepak spoke in a rehearsed manner and secretly checked his watch. Half an hour his father had said. "I must also go just now. I have an appointment in town."

"No, you don't, Deepak. Oh, don't look so shocked. Do you really think I know about your… friend here, but not the one in Soho? Don't be so naïve! There is a fine line between being a man of means, who occasionally dips into the honey pot and one who is addicted to whores."

Deepak Misra started to breathe again. Whores? So his father had no idea, who was waiting for him in town.

"Father, please…"

"You will go straight back to Reading. I'll give you a lift to Paddington Station and do not test me again, son. You will do the right thing for once and break it off with your lovers." Ashwin Misra turned around and walked back to the entrance. His driver was waiting patiently outside in the black limousine.

He liked life to be predictable and his son needed to toe the line once and for all.

"Yes father, as you wish." Deepak didn't know what else to say but he couldn't take the risk of the whole story being detected. He had to send a message that he was not coming. Today, he had to give his much other older lover a miss, but he would still pay the price. If his father only knew how forbidden this lover was. It filled him with hilarity. He turned away and grinned mischievously. Despite all the means at his father's disposal, he had not found out about that little detail?

Deepak didn't feel so despondent anymore. Toe the line, toe the line. That's all he'd ever heard since he'd been a boy. How boring his life would be without his lovers! And he was a grown man.

Father would not be able to keep a tail on him forever. They'd been down that road before. All he had to do was change his routine.

Ashwin Misra watched his son disappear into the train station with all the other people rushing up and down the broad stairs. When he'd lost sight of him, he took out his phone and rang his wife, who sat waiting in the large mansion in Reading, to tell her about the meeting with their unruly son.

"You are being too hard on the boy, Ashwin," Mrs. Misra complained to the man with whom she had spent 39 years of her life.

"He is hardly a little boy anymore or he would have already been given a hiding of sorts for carrying on the way he does. We can just hope that his bride will guide him in the right direction. We have the good family name to think of."

"But he's always been the quiet, sensitive one. He needs some freedom, Ashwin."

"Sensitive? Pah! How can I be too hard on him? He must learn to become a proper man. I just hope it's not too late. In any case, he is on his way home. I will be there later this evening. Now I must go to another meeting in London and I'm running late already. This boy is taking up too much of my time."

"Don't be too late, Ashwin. I'm making your favourite dhal dish." She had learnt how to appease her husband over the years.

"I won't be too late but I must leave now." Ashwin Misra sat in the back of his limousine, content with his efforts at being a good father. Nobody could accuse him of not trying his best.

"You know where to go," he said to his driver, and the car pulled off. His thoughts ran along familiar tracks, while he looked out of the window; not seeing how the classy townhouses in tree-lined avenues made space for cramped, spray-painted quarters in rubbish-strewn streets.

If the boy didn't toe the line, there were still other means at his disposal. Means, he usually reserved for his enemies. Deepak was his son after all and, his wife's favourite. If truth be told, that decision was still some way off. The boy would toe the line for a while at least. Ashwin Misra took a deep breath. It wasn't easy to be a good businessman, father, husband and upstanding member of society at all times.

Right now, he was looking forward to an hour of relaxation at a certain massage parlour where young, pretty things reminded him time and time again that he still had life in him and a right to his very own desires.

Their efforts would ease his headache and the heavy burden of responsibility he carried on his shoulders day in and day out.

Chapter SIX

"Please put your seat belts on, move your chair into an upright position and remain seated until the plane has come to a halt." The plane was about to land. Charlie nudged Lerato, who was napping next to her. "Wake up. We are here."

Lerato Gwala stared at her with big eyes and yawned.

"So that's it… we're in Port Elizabeth on official business," Charlie said and closed her seat belt with a click.

"Yes, we are," Lerato yawned.

The voice of the stewardess sounded stern. Her red-haired colleague rushed down the aisle to help a young man put a bag into the overhead-compartment and close it with a loud click.

He was strapped in and his seat moved to an upright position in no time before the stewardess pointed at somebody else. The red-haired stewardess nodded to offer a helping hand to a passenger at the back of the plane. Charlie closed her eyes as the plane tipped to the side and flew in a tight loop toward the tarmac of the landing strip. She opened her eyes and saw the expanse of the ocean right beneath them.

"Wow, look at that." Lerato was now wide awake.

"A little scary." Charlie grabbed the armrests hard. "Still can't believe I'm doing this. Why did I let you convince me to get involved in your case?" The airplane righted itself, aiming for the tarmac and she started breathing again.

"Because you have nothing better to do and it's a challenge you enjoy? It's a bit late to change your mind," she smiled.

"True."

"When we get to the guesthouse, we can figure out what to do in the next few days. But I want to go to the beach at some point. Just to relax." Lerato leaned back in her upright seat.

"I hear the beaches along Algoa Bay are stunning. Haven't you been here before?" The plane began its descent.

"We came here on holiday a few times with the family," Lerato said. "Even tried a spot of surfing with my brother. The beaches are stunning when it's not just after New Year's. It can be dangerous on Kings Beach with broken glass still lying around from all the revelling."

"So we are good. New Year is still a way off."

"There shouldn't be many tourists now."

"I like this town already."

Charlie put the headphones into the net on the chair in front of her. The landing gear made a knocking sound and minutes later, their plane touched down in Port Elizabeth. Charlie took off her jacket as they walked toward the car hire company.

This airport was tiny compared to OR Tambo in Johannesburg and it was so much warmer here. They drove their rental car to the guesthouse in the suburb of Humewood with the help of Google Maps and arrived at a fenced-in property.

"Secure parking! I like this," Lerato said while the gate hummed open.

The house resembled an Italian villa, complete with a Roman atrium inside. A swimming pool was surrounded by a roofed-in passage with heavy doors leading into the guest rooms. Everything was covered in lots of white and blue Delft tiles. Everywhere.

They took three blue-tiled steps up to the reception desk. A bright yellow suitcase was right in front of the reception, so they had to stand to the left and right of it. Charlie remembered seeing a bright yellow suitcase like that before.

"Welcome to Port Elizabeth," the stick-thin guesthouse owner said and sucked greedily on a glowing cigarette. "You must be Ms Gwala and Ms Proudfoot from Johannesburg."

"Yes, that's right," Lerato answered.

"I'm Mrs. Portwich, the owner of the guest house." Mrs. Portwich's crinkled lips released the cigarette. She picked up a pen and handed it to Charlie. "I see you like our tiles."

"Yes, it's very… impressive."

"Had them imported yonks ago. My husband adored European tiles. Good old James, he had such an eye for décor."

They put their names down in the guest book on the reception desk.

"Did you have a good flight?"

"Yes, thank you, hardly any turbulence," Charlie said and handed the pen to Lerato to sign the register.

"Are your eyes…?" Mrs. Portwich squinted at her.

"Yes, they are different colours," Charlie said patiently.

"Very unusual. Your room is down the passage on the right-hand side." The woman waved her free hand. "Don't worry. We're not prejudiced against couples like you. Not like some guesthouses. We have many people from all over the world come and stay with us. Especially from America, and we really don't mind. Careful when you go down the steps." Mrs. Portwich said all on one breath before taking another drag from her dwindling cigarette. She must have picked up on Charlie's slight American accent since she mentioned America.

"Mind what?" Charlie asked then got the woman's drift.

"Well, you know…"

"I'm afraid I don't. We are colleagues and came to PE for a work assignment. That's why we are sharing a room, being self-employed and all," Charlie lied a little just to stick it to the thin woman. Of course, she was talking about homosexual couples. And they were of a different race to boot. That must irk the owner of the guesthouse somewhat as she kept addressing Charlie and gave Lerato only fleeting looks.

"Ah well, no offence, ladies," Mrs. Portwich chattered on and snipped the ashes into the ceramic ashtray on the counter.

"None taken," Lerato said and smiled charmingly.

"There is a kettle in the room and coffee and tea bags, and a small fridge between the twin beds if you want to keep something to eat in there. I understand, being self-employed myself. You have your own shower. It's room no.2, the one with the blue curtains."

Charlie scanned the U-shaped passage. She quickly counted five rooms with windows facing the pool with curtains in dark green, blue, brown and purple.

"Breakfast is from 7 to 10 am every day by the swimming pool, and please… let me know in advance if you'd like to have lunch or dinner here at the guesthouse. Just so I can tell the cook, you know…"

The cigarette was right down to the filter. Mrs. Portwich stubbed it out in the ashtray and drew her lips into a smile that revealed stained teeth.

"Thank you, we'll do that," Lerato said and smiled back casually. "Could you give us the Wi-Fi password, please? We need to do some work later…"

"But of course…" The stick-woman scribbled on a pad and tore the small page off.

Lerato took the piece of paper and the key with a massive key tag. "Thank you kindly. We'll be off to our room now. We'll probably eat out tonight, not sure yet."

Charlie pulled out the handle of her suitcase and dragged it down the stairs and over the tiled floor to their room. The castors made a clattering noise, but the dark curtains stayed closed. "My, it is quite a bit warmer here than in Joburg," she said over the clatter.

"Yup, but it can get windy." Lerato stopped in front of the door with the brassy number 2 and opened the lock.

"Did you ever have to come to Port Elizabeth on official police business?"

"Not really. It had little to do with us in Cape Town. I just went on holiday with my family when I was in primary school. We played on the beach a lot …" Lerato reminisced. "So being here feels more like a holiday to me."

"A holiday sounds good to me…"

"We'll have to pull ourselves together and get

things done," Lerato said firmly. "That's what we are here for. Stop me if I want to go for a swim. We have more important things to do. Have you seen the connection cable for the laptop?"

She sat down on the bed by the window with a view of the swimming pool and tested the mattress. "Not too shabby."

"I think it's in the outside pocket of your tog bag." Charlie looked through the collection of teabags on the counter of the built-in kitchen "Do you want some tea?"

"To be honest, I feel more like a large bottle of cool drink right now."

"There it is." Charlie pointed to the loop of a black cable peeking out from one of the outside pockets of Lerato's bag. "The cable."

"There we go. Let me quickly set it up, then we can go to the shops and buy some supplies for our cute little fridgelet here." Lerato began to fiddle with the wall plugs.

"Phew, I'm glad I brought some short-sleeved tops with me. I'm dressed for winter in Joburg," Charlie said and opened her suitcase.

"The weather might still turn, but I doubt it will

get as cool as Joburg. Wind and rain more likely." Lerato plugged in the laptop and switched it on to check if everything worked as it should. "Good, let me connect to the Wi-Fi. Password. Done."

"Great," Charlie said and pulled a t-shirt over her head. "Let's go and find a shop, have a bite to eat and make a plan for tomorrow."

"I want to check out the Peele case before we pay the widower a visit. His wife was killed in an armed robbery at their fancy mansion high up on a hill, security and all. Couldn't find much in the public records online, but according to my client, Mr. Peele is from England and went to the same boarding school as Deepak Misra. I assume they were school friends."

"And our suspect was there when it happened?"

"We'll check that out. What we must do is find a connection. Who knows, we might just find out why the young husband would want to kill our Maribel-girl from Switzerland." Lerato put the print-outs of the e-mails on the desk and stood up. "All set. We have an address close to the new harbour. It's his office. So that's our first stop tomorrow."

"This client of yours has a lot of information."

"A good thing, too. Otherwise, we wouldn't have much to work with."

"Wait, that yellow trolley suitcase! I remember seeing it at the airport. It was on the luggage carousel for our flight." Charlie jumped off the bed.

"You mean the one by the reception desk?" Lerato asked.

"I don't know. There is something about that suitcase."

"Come on… there must be hundreds of suitcases just like that one in South Africa alone. What's so special about that one?"

"I don't know, I…"

"Hmm, your intuition kicking in already? Girl, you are worth every cent."

They heard Mrs. Portwich talking to a guest outside and the clatter of a trolley-suitcase passing by their room.

"Yes Mr. Misra, we have prepared everything just like the last time you were here. It's the room right at the back. Number 5."

The two women looked at each other. The owner of the guesthouse was having a conversation with someone called Mr. Misra! Could that be coincidence?

"You mean…?" Lerato whispered.

"Thank you so much, Mrs. Portwich." A young man answered in a polished British accent. "It's good to be back here. Much too warm in England this time of year."

"Soon, it will be quite a bit warmer here too," Mrs. Portwich said. "Not long now until the summer season starts."

"I hope I'll be gone by then," the young man answered. The noises grew fainter then stopped abruptly. A door opened. The young Englishman appeared to enter his room on the other side of the swimming pool. Lerato opened the dark-blue curtains just a crack to spy on the new arrival. The purple curtains on the far end of the passage were drawn close, so she could see only the shadow of the young man with the British accent.

"You have got to be kidding me!" Charlie said softly. "If it's the same guy, what is he doing here?"

"Do you recognise him from your dream?" Lerato looked amazed.

"His voice sounds just like him, but I don't know. I'd have to see his face to be sure."

"Room number 5. Chances are he hasn't seen us, either."

"What difference does it make? He doesn't know what I look like," Charlie said.

"True. I'm just glad he's not right next to our room. That would be creepy."

"Yes. Then why are you whispering?"

Lerato let go of the curtain. "Survival instinct, I guess. So you can't say for sure that you recognise his voice?"

"Not really, but a young guy with a British accent and that name? What are the odds, Lerato?"

"Shit. What is he doing here in this second-rate guesthouse? Mr. Misra is rich and can afford a five-star hotel in Summerstrand, right on the Marine Parade," Lerato said and checked the cash in her purse. "And then he comes here and, by the looks of it, not for the first time?"

They heard Mrs. Portwich speak to another new arrival at the entrance and a young woman soon moved into the room next to theirs.

"I have no idea. Maybe he doesn't want to be seen?" Charlie offered.

"Possibly. I see you're getting into the spirit of things."

The shower went on next door.

"Do you think it's a good idea to have breakfast in this place? We might bump into Mr. Misra here and blow our cover," Lerato said.

"What cover? Hold your horses. Maybe it's not even him… and if it is THE Mr. Misra, he has absolutely no idea who we are or that we are on his tail. He's never seen us before. It just feels like he knows me."

"So, what do you suggest we do? Act as if we've never heard of him and go about our business?" Lerato asked.

"Yes, what else? You are the detective." Charlie shrugged her shoulders.

"Well, this detective is hungry and thirsty, so let's find the nearest shopping centre and stock up."

"Alright then let's go." Charlie picked up her things.

"Andy said that he informed his contacts in the PE police force that we're coming to investigate. So, after our meeting with Mr. Peele tomorrow morning, we'll be off to see the investigating detective who was on the case three years ago before it was shelved. Andy gave me his phone number. Some guy called

Lennart van Rooyen. Ready to go to the shops and get supplies?"

"Ready when you are."

*

"Look at those kidneys, Lerato." Charlie stood at the breakfast buffet and heaped scrambled eggs and mushrooms on her plate. They had decided to confront the problem of this Mr. Misra being their suspect head-on, although it made Charlie uncomfortable.

"Try a couple of them. I'll get myself some of those tiny sausages."

Charlie helped herself to the fried kidneys and some hash browns.

"Jeepers, you are eating for an army, girl. Work is making you hungry."

"Only had a salad last night. Those sandwiches were laden with carbs and that's not good for me. But this I can eat."

"I keep forgetting about your sugar problem, but good for you that they had sugar-free cool drinks at that Spar. I'll try to remember to look out for low-carb stuff."

They had worked hard, searching the internet for

clues on the Peele case and their suspect and Lerato had kept working long after Charlie had gone to bed.

Should this mysterious Mr. Misra at their guesthouse indeed be the bridegroom in question, they would try and engage with him as little as possible, but they wanted to be sure. Mr. Peele's secretary had whatsapped to cancel the appointment and wanted to make new arrangements for later, so in about an hour they would pay a visit to the retired detective, who had investigated the Peele case at the time. With some luck, they would find out if there was a connection to their case.

"Good morning Mr. Misra, did you have a good night?" Mrs. Portwich greeted the English tourist who had just joined the others at the breakfast buffet.

"Yes thank you." There it was again, the voice. Their hostess moved on to the guests at the next table.

"Good morning Mr. and Mrs. Hansworth, going to the Oceanarium today as planned?" She chatted to the couple from Bloemfontein about dolphins, while Mr. Misra settled himself at a table next to the two women from Johannesburg.

Lerato couldn't avoid looking straight at him, but

Charlie wasn't ready to face 'her' possible killer.

"You look hungry doll, why don't you have some more bacon," Lerato winked at her friend. It took Charlie a moment to understand that Lerato wanted her to see the man's face from the safety of the buffet table.

"Ehem yes, I could eat a horse this morning," she said and stood up.

"Must be the good sea air." Lerato winked at her again and Charlie walked back to the buffet to get some bacon strips.

"Ah, Ms. Proudfoot, I'm glad you're enjoying our food." Mrs. Portwich intercepted Charlie at the buffet. Her conversation with the Hansworth couple had obviously ended and the guesthouse owner was on the prowl for more small talk.

"Yes, thank you Mrs. Portwich, the food is delicious."

"May I introduce you to Mr. Misra over here? He arrived yesterday from London via Johannesburg just after you did. My… you must have been on the same flight together!" The woman said cheerfully and Charlie froze.

Mrs. Portwich addressed Mr. Misra and nodded in Lerato's direction. "She is from America and is staying here with her partner for a few days…"

Charlie had no choice but to turn around and face the mysterious man. Deepak Misra nodded and smiled a greeting at the two women he had just been introduced to. Charlie's heart skipped a beat, but there was not even a glint of recognition in his eyes.

"Oh, I see. That's very interesting," he replied politely.

"Nice to meet you." Charlie didn't know what else to say to the killer she had seen in her dream. She tried to smile.

"Oh dear, we're almost out of bacon. I'll leave you to your breakfast," Mrs. Portwich said with an air of benevolence and went to the kitchen to organise more of the popular breakfast meat. Charlie cursed the woman's talkative nature.

"Are you here on vacation?" She asked Deepak Misra awkwardly.

"Well, I guess in a way I am," he said. "I'm visiting a friend. You?"

"Oh, we are here on a work assignment," Charlie answered and could have kicked herself. Oversharing! Lerato motioned for Charlie to come back to the table. At once! "Keep enjoying your stay Mr. Miller…"

"Misra is the name," Deepak corrected her. It had been an intentional error and it seemed to be working.

"Of course. Sorry about that, I'm not very good with names," she apologised. "Enjoy your stay in Port Elizabeth."

"And you too," Deepak Misra answered and laid into the buffet. He enjoyed bacon and all things carnivorous behind the back of his strictly vegetarian parents. He also liked a glass or two of whatever tipple was on offer and sometimes even other stimulants with his lovers.

"And?" Lerato lifted her chin in Deepak Misra's direction as Charlie approached. He stood with his back towards them, helping himself to the food on offer. Charlie nodded imperceptibly and sat down, trying to find her bearings. The encounter had rattled her. What now? Things like that just did not happen.

"Damn that old chatterbox, now he knows your name," Lerato whispered. "You need to learn not to overshare, doll. Can I have some of that bacon?"

"Sure, help yourself. I'm not really hungry anymore."

"More for me," Lerato tried to lighten the mood. "Come on, eat. It'll be a long day."

Charlie put some of the bacon and scrambled eggs in her mouth and chewed.

"I hope we can get another appointment with you-know-who for tomorrow," Lerato said and took out her phone. "Hopefully the man is in town. You never know with those super-rich guys."

"I guess we'll find out soon enough." Charlie finished the last bit of her scrambled eggs and whispered, "so did you find out anything interesting about the Peele case?"

"Not as cut and dried as it appeared." Lerato gave her friend a quick update in a subdued voice, acting as if they were talking about a completely different matter. "And now I'll have some of that bacon." They both laughed.

Deepak Misra walked past their table and gave the two women a cold smile.

*

Grey-haired Lennart van Rooyen had retired since the Peele murder case went cold last year. It was one of the last two cases he'd worked and it still weighed on his conscience that he'd not been able to resolve it. The former detective sergeant was getting a bit hard of hearing, but he was a friendly enough fellow and didn't seem to mind answering their questions.

"I'll do what I can if you just manage to find the killer of that poor lady," he said and offered them sweet lemonade. Charlie declined and asked for some water. The retired detective went to the kitchen to fetch a glass for her.

"What's your take on him?" Lerato asked her while he was out of sight.

"I think he's leaving out bits and pieces of the puzzle," Charlie whispered just as he showed up again.

"That's what I think," Lerato said in a normal voice.

"What do you think, Ms Gwala?" The elderly man asked.

"That we'll also do our best, Mr. van Rooyen."

"Thank you. I still regret that I couldn't take the guy, who'd robbed the Peeles into custody."

"So, you still believe that her death was an accident?"

Lerato had taken over the conversation, being the former policewoman. Lerato asked the questions and Charlie mostly listened. "The reason why we are here is that we might have reason to suspect foul play."

"You don't say," the ex-detective said and put the glass on the table in front of Charlie. Some of the water spilled onto the table cloth.

"Yes well, we are investigating a possible connection to this case with another murder," Lerato said.

"Are you now?" Mr. van Rooyen made a gruff noise and sat down on the couch.

They had agreed upfront not to divulge any details regarding the nature of their own investigation. You could never be sure where the information would end up, even if they were dealing with a connection of her partner, Andy Malherbe.

"Could you run us through the case, Mr. van Rooyen?"

"Please call me Lennart."

"Very well, Lennart. Did anything about Mrs. Peele's death strike you as unusual?" Lerato probed.

He gave them an account of how the victim's husband and closest friends had been questioned first and ruled out as suspects, although the evidence was ambiguous. Jewellery theft in high places was not exactly news. She already knew about the records on the case, but wanted to verify what she'd researched.

"Have some biscuits," Lennart van Rooyen offered. The biscuits in a glass bowl on the table looked a little iffy.

"No, thank you. What is it that Mr. Peele does for a living?" Lerato asked and took a sip of her lemonade.

"Oh, he's a businessman of sorts like so many others, I suppose. Import-export. Came up in a number of other investigations into white-collar crime, but we couldn't make the evidence stick. Covered his tracks well, or rather, his accountant did."

"You don't seem to like the man very much," Charlie stated.

"Not if I can help it."

"Right. Do you think Mrs. Peele's murder might have something to do with his business connections?" Lerato asked.

"We followed that trail, of course. There was just so little to go on. Even the staff at the mansion were not giving us much. Pretty useless as witnesses."

"The staff at the mansion? That would be the butler and driver, the housekeeper and laundry maid?"

"As far as I remember." Van Rooyen didn't seem too sure.

"What about the neighbours? They must have heard something."

"Nothing," he confirmed.

"Did you question the staff at Mr. Peele's office?"

"Well, yes we did, but they had obviously been briefed to answer in a certain way and seemed quite scared to speak to us. If I were you, I wouldn't even go there." The question made him visibly uncomfortable. His answer seemed a little like a warning. It was evident that they were getting close.

"Do you think that's also true for the staff at the Peele mansion?"

"They never heard a thing that day. Nobody had come in or left the house. So I ask you, how was it done? Did the perp escape through a secret passage or dive into the ocean from the top floor? Although, that would have been a miracle if you ask me. He would have cracked his head on the rocks below for sure."

"If that was true - that there is a secret passage - wouldn't the husband have to be involved somehow? I mean how likely is it that a random robber would know how to leave the house unseen through a secret passage?"

"I suppose so, but it's only a vague possibility. Mr. Peele was on a business trip in Durban at the time of the murder. We had to rule him out. Mr. Peele was not a prime suspect because of his absence. What exactly is it that you are investigating?"

"The connection between two cases, sir." Lerato kept her answer as vague as possible. "Could it have been a paid killer, perhaps?"

"We did consider that option. But, it's one thing to have a hunch and quite another to have the necessary proof. First, we decided that it must have been a robbery gone wrong. Jewellery was stolen from a leather-bound box in Sarah Peele's bedroom, but a brand-new laptop and state of the art electronic equipment were left untouched. But in the end, as you must know, Mrs. Peele's death was ruled an accident. Poor lady shot herself with her husband's gun."

"A jewellery theft takes some planning, doesn't it? Were any pieces of jewellery recovered from pawnshops or the like?"

"We checked out pawnshops in the area, alas without luck."

"That's odd. So it wasn't a random crime, then."

"We don't know that. The lady of the house must have surprised the thief and he silenced her, but we couldn't prove it," Mr. van Rooyen offered.

"Why not just tie her up and leave with the loot through said secret passage?"

"We don't know that there is a secret passage. We never found one. Perhaps our victim started making a fuss and needed to be silenced or she recognised the perpetrator. Or she actually shot herself, because she didn't know how to handle the weapon. The only fingerprints we found belonged to Mrs. Peele."

"Possible, but is it likely? That's the question. Is there anything else of interest about the case you could share with us?"

"Such as?"

"How was Mrs. Peele murdered?" Lerato knew, of course, that the killer had shot the woman but she wanted to hear it from the detective's lips. He thought for a long moment.

"I truly don't believe that she shot herself, but there is no proof of third party interference. Mrs. Peele fired her husband's gun, conceivably at the fleeing robber. The bullet, a 9mm Parabellum, penetrated her face under her left eye and exited through her right upper skull. The report says that the weapon jammed and she turned it around to look at the bore. Then the weapon must have accidentally gone off. At least that was the conclusion by the ballistics expert. There was, unfortunately, no evidence that could prove otherwise." He shrugged his shoulders, growing visibly uncomfortable as if they had inadvertently accused him of something.

"That's an unusual theory, don't you think?" Lerato said.

"In a way, yes I suppose you could say that. To my mind, it's possible that the robber made it look like an accident. It looked more like a professional hit to me. Mrs. Peele did not have a lover or stalker or family member with any grudge against her. Her maiden name was Dubey or Dooley; something like that. She had no relatives here in PE in any case. They were all overseas."

"So nobody was visiting at the time of her death?"

"We had no evidence that anybody else was in the house, except for the butler and the maid. Her family lives in England and she kept to herself. We were unable to find a suspect. The butler and the maid had no motive."

"So, you believe it could've been a professional hit?" Charlie asked.

"Well, if it was a robbery and the poor woman was a casualty, it couldn't have been. But who knows." He spilled a little of his lemonade on the table cloth. "It's all very difficult to prove."

"Who found the victim?"

"The butler. He said he heard a sharp sound on the second floor and went to investigate. Found Mrs. Peele lying on the floor in the bedroom. She died before the ambulance arrived."

"Shame, poor woman. She must've looked a sight," Lerato said.

"Did the name Misra ever pop up during your investigation?" Charlie asked on a whim and the answer surprised both women.

"In fact yes. A Mr. Misra from Reading in England had been visiting Mr. Peele just before he flew off to Durban on business. It's in the original report..."

"Really?" Lerato hadn't seen any mention of their suspect's name. Their clue had come from the client in England.

"We checked with the staff at the mansion. They seemed reluctant to share any information, but since Mr. Misra seemed to have overnighted at a hotel or such, they had brought up his name.

He had been there before and usually used one of the guest rooms on the first floor. Alas, he left Port Elizabeth just before the incident and arrived in England on the day of the murder. We were unable to establish his whereabouts or an exact time of departure from South Africa. His name didn't come up in the passenger lists. Happens sometimes. Bad luck."

"You don't say. That's very odd." Lerato was disappointed. This put a damper on their theory that Deepak Misra might have carried out the murder himself, as the e-mails, Mrs. Sharma had forwarded, suggested.

"Another suspect down the drain," she sighed. "But thank you for speaking to us so frankly, Mr. van Rooyen."

"I'm sorry I can't be of more help to you."

"Well then, who were your prime suspects in the case?" Lerato Gwala asked.

"That's the baffling thing about the case. We couldn't come up with any prime suspects. The woman's two friends insisted that Mr. Peele had a motive because he was allegedly unfaithful to his wife and tried to avoid a 50/50 split in case of a divorce. There was also some bad blood between Mrs. Peele and her family in England. They refused to collaborate with the police and none of them had ever spent time with the couple in Port Elizabeth. I'm told that they were not on speaking terms." He shrugged his shoulders.

"Are you saying that Mrs. Peele wanted to divorce her husband?"

"She had already seen a lawyer about a potential divorce arrangement. That's motive and would make Mr. Peele our no.1 suspect, but we were going around in circles because he was not even in town at the time of the murder. No paper trail of any unusual payments from his account to a potential gunman. Only a business deal with Mr. Misra around that time. A dead-end. The death was ruled accidental, end of story. Nothing further we could do. Unless new evidence comes to light, the conclusion by the ballistics expert stands."

"Well, I suppose you are right and it might be a

dead-end," Lerato played things down. "Thank you very much for your help, Mr. van Rooyen. Is there a way we could inspect the actual police docket on the case?"

"I wish I could organise it for you but the docket disappeared together with three others from a filing cabinet at the court archive a few months ago. That's not the first time this has happened and it won't be the last, I'm afraid."

He looked around, playing nervously with the tissue he had used to dab up the lemonade he had spilled.

"Insider job?" Charlie piped up.

"Certainly not!" The retired police detective sergeant seemed annoyed at the insinuation and threw the crumpled up tissue onto the table.

"No offence, sir," Lerato apologised and shot Charlie a wilting look.

"None taken. If that'll be all... I do hope you'll catch your perpetrator." The ex-detective seemed somewhat impatient now. He picked up the glasses and the lemonade jug. "If you don't mind I've got things to do."

"So do we," Lerato smiled sweetly and got up. "We are done here. Thank you very much for the information you provided. I'll be sure to give Andy your best."

They said their good-byes and the two sleuths drove down to the beach to talk about their visit with the retired policeman. It was only a stone's throw away from the detective's house.

"What were you thinking? You can't rile up my contacts like that," Lerato chided Charlie. "We were lucky to get to speak to him at all." They walked on the sand not far from the road.

"Sorry, I didn't know that I was doing that. But he didn't give us much, just tiptoed around the murder. No evidence other than a hare-brained ballistics report? It makes kind of sense that the police docket disappeared, doesn't it?" They sat down on a rock in the shade of a shrub at the edge to the beach.

"I don't mean to be harsh, Charlie. It's just the guy was hiding information from us and he seemed a little short-tempered when you asked him about the insider job. I thought I could get more out of him. That's why you have to tread carefully. The police force is not immune to corruption, you know." Lerato played with her car keys. "We don't have much to go on and how are we supposed to connect Deepak Misra to this case if he left before the robbery even went down?"

"Did you bring me down to PE because of my pretty face or because of my so-called talent of intuition? There are still other scenarios," Charlie said somewhat annoyed. "Don't lose those keys in the sand, Lerato or we'll be in trouble."

Lerato put the keys into her purse. "Do you mean that Lennart van Rooyen is somehow involved?"

Charlie nodded. "I'm not sure how, but he was certainly lying when he told us about the police docket."

"So he wasn't just embarrassed, because he messed up the case. And he's Andy's contact or friend or whatever you want to call it."

They got up and walked silently side by side, sitting down again closer to the water's edge. The steady sound of the surf had something soothing about it. After a while, the surf came nearly up to their feet.

"Andy obviously didn't know," Charlie said. "Look, it doesn't mean that the guy was involved in the killing or any other crime or that he won't help us. He just knows more than he's letting on. Even if he's not the worst policeman on the planet, he knows who stole the docket."

"Maybe." Lerato felt downhearted. "He's definitely not giving us the whole story and that's suspicious. Maybe we should pay the Clerk of the Court a visit and check Lennart's story out."

"Sure. At least we have confirmation that this Misra guy was here just before the gig went down at the Peele house. There's your connection," Charlie said.

"The theory that Mrs. Peele killed herself by accident is absolute rubbish. We should keep digging. Our suspect could have helped organise the robbery and killing. Maybe the robbery was a cover for Mrs. Peele's murder? Irritating that he stays at our guest house. I wonder why he's in town."

"Business?" Charlie dug her toes into the sand.

"Just what kind of business? It'll be difficult to tail Misra and keep up with the items on our to-do-list."

"We'll just keep plugging away at it. Did you hear from Peele's secretary?"

Lerato scoffed. "She sent me a message while we were at Lennart's house. Meeting's arranged for tomorrow morning at 11 o'clock at some pizza joint right up the road from here. Donatello's. Never heard of it."

"Maybe it's a new restaurant. Why are we not meeting at his office?"

"He thinks I'm here for business. Maybe he wants to go for brunch."

"At a pizza place? Hmmm. So you didn't tell him why we are here?"

"No, I thought it would be better to tell him when we meet."

"As long as I meet him face to face, I might get an idea if he was involved in his wife's murder or our friend, Deepak Misra," Charlie said.

"It's all guesswork at this stage, so do your magic with Peele tomorrow."

"Magic – I'm a magician now." Charlie let the sand squish between her toes as she watched a group of surfers out in the ocean riding crashing waves in the distance. The sea breeze picked up and grains of sand prickled on their legs.

"To me you are. But how do we get proof?" Lerato moaned. "It's really important that we prove a connection between Mr. Misra and this case. Maybe the guy is a psychopath or maybe my client is trying to pull one over on him."

"We don't need proof that Peele was involved. I mean we are not solving this cold case. All we have to do is save the life of his future wife. It feels like a puzzle that doesn't make sense just yet. We just have to go with our gut and put the pieces together."

A couple walked past, holding hands and Charlie's heart skipped a beat.

"Alright, let's not get carried away. I suppose we should focus on what we have," Lerato said. "I just wish I could solve this case and question our Misra guy while he's under my nose. Two birds with one stone."

"Maybe the police will open the case again. You can always give them the evidence we find. Because you're not with the police anymore, remember?"

"Right… I haven't read all of the mails yet, but they are pretty explicit. Along the lines of 'how much are you willing to pay' and 'we'll both lay her to her rest' and stuff like that. Mainly two recipients."

"The pictures I've seen were pretty disturbing, but Deepak in BDSM gear doesn't mean he's connected to this murder case. It just raises doubt about the upcoming marriage," Charlie heaved a sigh.

"I'm not even sure that they could be used in court if push comes to shove."

"Great. Can't you contact Maribel's aunt? Maybe she has more proof," Charlie asked and tickled her toes with a leafy branch she'd picked up.

"I could, I suppose. Something linking him to a hitman for example, not just to Robert Peele. I believe that that's who our recipients are."

"I'm sure that Andy can research that for us. For now, we could drive up to the Peele mansion and see if we can find that secret passage Lennart was talking about." Charlie suggested.

"Snooping around that place? There are probably a million security cameras, not to speak of the staff at the house and suspicious neighbours. And if the police haven't found a passage, then how could we?" Lerato objected feebly.

"You never know." Charlie stood up, put her shoes back on and dusted the fine sand off her rolled-up trousers. "At the very least, I'll get a feel of the place. That's what you want me to do, right? We can always say we lost our way and were looking for a different address. That's not unheard of, is it?"

"Hmm, daring. I like that," Lerato said and grabbed her purse. "You're getting into the spirit of things."

"Doing my best, Madam Private Investigator." Charlie grinned. "Wouldn't want you to waste your money on a useless consultant. We came here to do a job and that's what we are going to do."

"My kind of girl," Lerato chuckled. They walked toward the road and scanned the shops behind the parked cars on the Marine Parade. "Let's have some lunch, then we'll be off to the courthouse and then we can take a drive up the hill."

"Lunch?" Charlie looked confused.

"Yes, as in eating food. I'm starving," Lerato said. "And shouldn't you keep your blood sugar levels constant?"

"You're right. I always forget to eat," Charlie admitted.

"Not on my watch… I feel like seafood. Surely, there must be seafood to be had around here."

"Are you kidding? There are plenty of restaurants. We are right on the coast. Let's eat quickly and then get back to work."

"I see the investigating bug has bitten you," Lerato laughed at her friend's eagerness. "And I'm certainly not complaining."

Chapter SEVEN

They stuck to their simple plan. First, a seafood platter at a small place on the Marine Parade, then a visit to the Clerk of the Court. Afterwards, they drove up to the Peele mansion, on a hill outside of town. It took the better part of twenty minutes as the wind from the ocean was blowing up against the car.

The search at the court house hadn't turned up anything new. Another dead end. The docket of the Peele case had disappeared together with other dockets a year after the investigations had been concluded. Just as Lennart had told them.

"Damp squib," Lerato said as they got into the car. "That trip cost us more than an hour. Perhaps we'll have more luck feeling out the mansion on the hill."

"I think it will," Charlie had to shout because a couple of motorbikes roared past.

The drive was pleasant and after every bend on the coastal road with stark cliffs and beaches, the holiday-feeling became stronger. They could almost forget the reason why they were in this affluent neighbourhood.

Lerato parked the vehicle some way down in a side road and discovered a footpath that led around the top of the hill just underneath the grandiose Peele mansion and a neighbouring property. "Here we are, going up the hill. Do your magic, Charlie."

Surprisingly, the u-shaped footpath was open to the public. Tourists could pick their way around the jagged rocks underneath the overhanging rock face to the small gate on the other side.

As Lerato had predicted, there were plenty of security cameras on every property in the street, but strangely enough, no cameras or electric fences hampered their inspection of the rocky terrain below the two mansions. It didn't seem very popular as there was nobody else around.

"Interesting that there is a public footpath," Lerato stated laconically. She inspected the small gate and the sign stated that no littering or swimming was permitted. But because the beach was virtually inaccessible from here, nobody would come up all this way to go swimming on the beach.

"But somebody could try to abseil down here or climb up with the right gear," Charlie suggested.

"The police would have found some trace of that, I'm sure. Just look at that view!"

Lerato took a deep breath and caught up with her friend. Charlie couldn't be bothered with the view. She studied the lay of the land.

"Looks like the rocks are too jagged to climb and they have security to rival Fort Knox up there, but I guess it's possible," she said.

"So how the hell did this jewel thief slash killer get into the house in the first place? Was he a cat burglar and then abseiled into the jagged rocks to get away?"

"Must have been some kind of ninja."

Lerato glanced up and estimated the drop to be around 30 meters. Climbing would have been no easy feat and not the fastest option to get in and out of the mansion. "With the danger of getting speared on the rocks, especially in the dark, it seems more likely that someone let him into the house. It's possible that the staff were lying to the police. So either that or he climbed the rocks or there is a secret passage, just as Lennart suspected. So let's see…"

"What makes you so sure that our perp was a he? Could have just as well been a female thief..." Charlie lifted her eyebrows.

"True, but shooting somebody in the face is not exactly a female way to off someone. Then again, we can't be sure of anything. Are you getting some kind of whiff that it might have been a woman or what?"

"Hey, I'm not a sniffer dog, and not everything I say is a hunch or proof of anything. Sometimes I just have an idea," Charlie snarled at her.

"Alright, alright. I'm just hoping for something concrete for a change," Lerato replied. "All we have is speculation about virtually everything. So, that seems to be the other end of the crescent path." She shrugged her shoulders and walked towards the road.

"Let's walk back then. Maybe we missed something," Charlie said and tied her hair up with an elastic to keep it from being blown about by the wind. "Don't you think it's odd that nobody has pitched up to ask what we are doing here? I mean with all those security cameras pointing at us."

"Maybe we are not the first tourists to have discovered this view of the ocean." Lerato shielded her eyes with her hand and looked out to sea. "All we need is a bench and we have a proper destination for an outing."

"Yup, when it's not so windy," Charlie grumbled.

They looked up at the steep rock face and checked behind boulders for clues, while the rushing sounds of the ocean and the wind accompanied their efforts.

"If there is such a thing as a secret passage around here, it's extremely well hidden." Lerato looked disappointed and sat down on a flat rock half-way around to the other side where they had started their investigation.

"Just look at that view!" She said while Charlie was still knocking against rocks here and there.

She suddenly realised that her friend was no longer next to her. "Charlie? Where are you?" Lerato called. There was no answer. "Charlie?"

"I'm over here." Charlie had slipped through the narrow space between two boulders and stood behind a gnarled tree right by the overhang.

"Where? I can't see you." Lerato stood up and searched in the direction of Charlie's voice, but there was no sign of her.

"Look up here!" Charlie stepped forward onto the ledge, grinning broadly. "I think I found it. Not bad, is it?"

"How did you get up there?" Lerato was dumbfounded.

"Aha! I used the entrance down there," she said triumphantly. "Is that concrete enough for you?"

"I'm having kittens," Lerato said. She found the narrow space and slipped through it. "Is that… what I think it is?"

She inspected a low door that pointed away from the path and was disguised by the small tree.

"Close your mouth," Charlie chuckled and disappeared from the ledge. Seconds later, she opened the entrance to the secret passage.

"Hey, don't get cheeky with me, young lady," Lerato teased her. "Remember, who is running this investigation?"

"Sssshh." Charlie put a finger over her lips. "Do you see the stairs at the back?"

"No."

"You must stand right in front of the door." She put her finger against her lips and whispered. "I think there's a camera up there."

"What?" Lerato mouthed.

"A camera. The door is open and there are steps leading up to the ledge, then through an artificial tunnel," Charlie whispered. "Pretty good camouflage."

"Damn!" Lerato took a few pictures of the open door, the stairs and the ledge with her cell phone. "Why didn't the police find it? Someone didn't even bother to lock the door." They were still whispering and tried to turn away from the camera as much as possible. Although it was improbable, somebody might be watching them. It was too late to disable the device.

"We nearly didn't find it," Charlie muttered.

"So what made you look there?"

"I'll tell you on the way back. I don't have a good feeling about this place and not just because of the camera up there." They were still whispering. She pulled her friend back towards the boulders in front of the ledge. They both ducked for a few moments and Lerato snapped more pictures from her new perspective.

"Then let's rather get out of here," Lerato said and pointed toward the road. "I think I've got what I need."

They sneaked along the outside of the boulders

and walked inconspicuously along the uneven path. As soon as they were in the road, they began to chat like tourists, who didn't have a care in the world. They got into their rental car and carefully made their way down the serpentine road past green gardens, luxury flats and mansions. The wind from the sea seemed to be dying down in the afternoon.

"Lennart van Rooyen was right," Lerato blurted out as she negotiated a particularly narrow curve. "But some sloppy police work, I must say! Why didn't they listen to him and search a little harder? It's proof that somebody knew full well how to get into the house and out without being seen."

"Explains a lot," Charlie said and admired the view of the ocean until they'd reached the next turn. She was more relaxed now that they had left the eerie place.

"You think not even the neighbours know about the door?" Lerato wondered.

"They probably never use the path and maybe it's usually locked?"

"If the police couldn't find that door three years ago during their investigations - honestly, that's so weak - how did you know where to look?"

"You won't believe it if I told you," Charlie said on a sigh and rolled up the window.

"Try me." Lerato looked at her sideways. "I know you better than that."

"Okay… well, somebody showed it to me."

"What? You're pulling my leg! There was nobody else around." Lerato was so surprised that she swerved a little into the road.

"I told you, you wouldn't believe me." Charlie rolled her eyes.

"No seriously?! I didn't see anybody. Zero."

"There was nobody else but us around. At least not in that sense. I saw a… a woman, or the shape of a woman. More like smoke or mist. Well anyway, she kind of swirled something like an arm out and toward the door up there."

"She did? And you knew to look there?"

"Yes. Now you can call me crazy or psychic or whatever you like." Charlie crossed her arms in defiance.

"You think… it might be the ghost of the dead woman?" Lerato whispered.

"I don't know what it was."

"I told you that you have a gift…" Lerato began.

"Oh come on. That's never happened to me before."

"…of intuition," Lerato finished her sentence. Somehow it felt wrong to still call it that. To her mind, Charlie was not just intuitive, but downright psychic.

"What has swirling smoke got to do with intuition?"

"I don't know! What else would you call it?"

A luxury car drove up the road and narrowly passed them. Lerato decided to pay attention to where she was going and soon they were back on the main road and on their way back into town. They didn't notice a battered car following them down the hill that came closer and closer. The car was dirty brown and blended into the background of the hill. When Lerato eventually looked up and checked the rear mirror, she creased her forehead in disbelief and grunted.

"What's up?" Charlie asked.

"What the hell is this guy doing?" Lerato grumbled and held up her middle finger when the car attempted to overtake them and dinged the bumper of their rental car.

"Wow, wait a minute… did you see what that moron just did?" Lerato asked angrily.

"I did! Is he trying to run us off the cliff or what?"

Charlie turned, but couldn't see the driver. There was another light impact.

Lerato came dangerously close to the edge of the road, swung the steering wheel around, scraping along the steep cliffside. The surface was slippery with loose gravel and sand and the vehicle slid back onto the tar road.

"Hey!"

"Be careful!" Charlie yelled. For a brief moment, she had seen the surf on the rocks below. She grabbed onto the dashboard and the door at the same time, as if it would save her in case they fell off the cliff.

"I am being careful, but this idiot is not!" Lerato swerved away from the edge and put her foot on the gas to get away from their attacker. The brown car fell behind but closed the gap again after a few seconds.

Suddenly the leisurely drive along the coastal road had turned into a race for their lives. The offending car caught up with them and scratched against the back of the rental car, knocking it forward. Lerato was furious by now.

"Bloody, f**king asshole!" She shouted. "Who is this idiot?"

"He's doing it on purpose for sure. But why?" Charlie cried. She turned around again, but all she could make out through the tinted car windows was the vague silhouette of a man in the driving seat. "It's some guy in a hoodie. Why the hell is he driving so fast?"

"Who cares, we need to get away from that damn idiot!" The car caught up with them again. Lerato managed somehow to keep theirs steady, but it began to slide onto the loose sand again. The dirty-brown car didn't budge from their back and came even closer. A small truck whistled past on the other side of the road.

"We are too close to the edge. Put your foot down and move to the inside of the road." Charlie tried to say it calmly but her voice got the better of her.

Lerato put her foot down on the gas pedal, gaining a larger gap on the pursuing car and swung the steering wheel around into the road. A sports car hooted and overtook them. "Don't you see what's going on? Self-involved, rich, bloody…" She swore and lost her train of thought.

"I wish we had a sports car right now." Charlie hung onto the dashboard.

They now had more company on the road. A 4x4 headed straight for them. They both shrieked and Lerato altered course. The rental car moved outward toward the edge of the cliff again and the 4x4 screeched past, hooting like mad. Their pursuer had been hanging back but the car came closer now.

"Bloody hell! That guy won't stop running us off the cliff!" Lerato shouted. She looked in the rear mirror for a split second.

"F**king bastard! Can't you go any faster, Lerato?" Charlie shrieked frantically as the brown car fell back a little only to accelerate again.

"Charlie, it's a rental, not a sports car! But that thing doesn't look much better. How can he get so much power out of that rattletrap?" Going into another curve, Lerato tried to get away from the edge, nearly ramming a blue car. The driver hooted angrily and hung back, giving their pursuer a chance to get closer again.

"Look! Is that a police car coming up the hill?" Charlie bellowed.

"Could be… why?" Lerato yelled back.

"Why?! It's a police car, dammit! Flash them!"

"What?"

"Not like that. Get your head out of the gutter! Switch your headlights on and off. We have to be in their face or they won't see us!"

Lerato switched the headlights on and off and their car wobbled back into the middle of their lane. The banged-up vehicle was still in close pursuit, but had obviously spotted the police car as well. "Why don't they put their siren on? Are they used to speeding cars around here?"

"Lean on the hooter! Do it!" Charlie yelled at her.

Lerato leaned on the hooter. It made a dreadful noise and, at last, the police vehicle seemed to react, switched on its headlights and then the sirens.

"Finally!" There was relief in Lerato's frenzied voice. "Where is that damn asshole now?" The asshole overtook the rental car, nearly ramming the oncoming police vehicle in the process and zoomed downhill, around the next curve and was out of sight.

Lerato took her foot off the gas pedal and slammed on the brakes.

Their car came to a screeching halt between the yellow line and the edge, slipping a little on loose gravel. They needed to catch their breath and so did their car.

"Damn close shave!" Lerato gasped.

"Yeah, damn close!" Charlie agreed. She was panting as if she'd run a marathon.

The police vehicle reversed down to the spot where Lerato and Charlie had parked on the gravel. Two police officers exited the vehicle, talking animatedly to each other. The policewoman in the driver's seat called the incident in, while a stout policeman opened the door on the passenger side and walked across the sloping road, slowing down two hooting cars with hand movements.

"Ladies, what was that all about? Are you alright?" He asked and Lerato gave him a breathless account of their ordeal in Xhosa before switching back to English for Charlie's benefit.

"You were going at quite a speed. Did you have anything to drink?"

"NO, we had nothing to drink. I told you: the brown car was chasing us and tried to run us off the cliff. That's why I was going so fast. If I was drunk, I wouldn't have tried to get your attention!"

The policeman grunted and saw how Lerato's hands trembled as she released her grip from the steering wheel.

"Sorry, we are quite upset." She tried to keep her hands still and took a deep breath. "He nearly succeeded."

"And you say you saw a man in that brown car?" The policeman didn't seem completely convinced by her story.

"Yes, I saw it when I turned around to check what was going on," Charlie confirmed Lerato's story with animated gestures. "Please officer, try to find this guy."

He grunted again. "Can you give us the car license number or a description of what the driver looked like?"

"I don't think he had a license plate and frankly, we tried to stay alive. So no, I did not have a good look at that number or the man. The windscreen and windows were tinted and we just saw that it was a man in a hoodie."

"It was a Nissan Pulsar. Older model. Souped-up. Wouldn't raise an eyebrow in a township, but it had enough power to keep up with us all the way," Lerato added.

"We could see that it was a Nissan. My colleague

radioed the description of the car through to the call centre. Hopefully, we'll be able to pick him up soon. Could be a drunk driver. There are too many of them on this road."

"Yeah, like that's going to happen," Lerato whispered to Charlie.

The policeman didn't seem too concerned. He took off his peaked hat and pulled his pants up by the belt. The policewoman joined them and gave the two women a suspicious once-over. Her colleague repeated what Lerato and Charlie had told him and the woman's stare softened a little.

"We weren't sure what was going on. If you were drunk or what. Maybe the other driver tried to hijack your car. We still have to do a breathalyser test on you."

"If you must…" Lerato sighed and breathed into the tube. It was better to comply. "As long as you catch that lunatic."

The policewoman walked over to Charlie's side and repeated the test.

"And?" Lerato asked in a bored tone.

"You are clear."

"Good thing you made a noise and flashed your

headlights. Good thing, you kept your car on the road," her colleague said to Lerato and frowned at the rental car. "How did you learn to drive a car like that? We saw you hurtling down the road from up there."

"Advanced driver's course." Lerato gave him a weak smile and he nodded his head in appreciation. "Poor car took a bit of a hammering."

"Would you like to make an official statement about the circumstances of the incident?" A car raced past them and the police officers looked up, shaking their heads. They said something in Xhosa, then decided to ignore the speeding driver.

"We might need a case number," Lerato said. "Just in case there's something wrong with the car. I'll have to report what happened to the rental company."

"No problem. You can follow us to the station. We can do a full statement there."

"Thank you, officer," Charlie breathed more easily now.

The two police officers got back into their vehicle and turned around. Lerato followed them at a normal speed. They had somewhat recovered from the incident on the coastal road and by the time they made it back to town, the ocean was engulfed in a picturesque sunset. Lerato filled in forms at the police station and answered questions at the same time.

"Do you have an idea why this driver wanted to run you off the road?"

"Actually, I do," Lerato said and filled in the date on the form. The policewoman was amazed. There was an answer she didn't get every day.

"Oh really? Do you want to tell us?"

Lerato sighed. "I am a private investigator. We are in PE to investigate a suspect linked to a cold case. Then it turned out that the case might not be as cold as we thought. That's the explanation I have."

The policewoman stared at her. "Hai wena!"

"Unless it was a drunk driver," Lerato continued, "which I doubt very much, it's more likely that there is a connection to the not so cold case. I'm sorry, I should introduce myself." Lerato took out her PI badge. "I am Lerato Gwala, private detective from Joburg, and former detective sergeant with the Cape Town Police Force. This is my associate Ms Proudfoot, also from Joburg."

"You are from Johannesburg?" A stocky police officer had overheard the conversation. "Are you with the police?"

"No, we're not. We are with the Maitirelo PI Agency. Well, as I said, we are working a cold case here in Port Elizabeth and had a meeting with Lennart van Rooyen this morning. He is the retired detective, who was on the Sarah Peele case three years ago. We discussed it with him and followed up on a clue."

"Ah yes, I see." The officers remembered the case well. The scandal had rocked their town. "Good old Lennart," the stocky officer said. "And the American lady here?"

"I'm a consultant and South African, but my parents moved to America when I was a child." She answered and gave them a charming smile.

"Oh, white folks who are afraid of staying in the new South Africa?"

The remark was offensive, but Lerato had just the right answer. "My associate here was adopted by black parents. And they moved to America for their own reasons."

"Hai wena!" The police officers stared at each other and couldn't think of a comeback. Eventually, the policewoman roused herself. "So, you're saying this driver doesn't want you to investigate? Did you receive a threat?"

"No, we just had a look at the surroundings of the crime scene. We didn't even go near the mansion or see anyone else there."

The two police officers had a brief discussion and again Lennart van Rooyen's name was mentioned. A few times.

"We can't help you with the cold case but we'll give you a case number for the car insurance," The policeman said. "Maybe old Lennart has an idea if this tailgating has to do with your case. Possible that somebody found out about your visit and followed you."

"Well, we never even spoke to anyone, not to stir things up," Charlie said. "So I don't know how he could have found out, but you never know."

"Call came in. An incident in Bakkies Road. Domestic violence."

Another officer approached them. "Crap! That's the road where old Lennart lives. I'll go with Gumede." The sturdy officer said, then turned to Lerato. "Sign your statement. You can come to his house with us. Maybe he knows what's going on with your case."

"Thank you, officer," Lerato said. "Can you give me the case number, please?"

They drove in convoy to Lennart van Rooyen's house as the sun was only a whisper above the dark horizon. As they got closer to Bakkies Road, an ambulance flashed its lights and rushed past them.

Another emergency vehicle and a police car were parked outside the modest home they had visited this morning. "What's going on? Something must have happened at Mr. van Rooyen's house."

"I hope he didn't have a heart attack. Didn't look too well, earlier," Lerato said.

"If he was taken away by an ambulance, he is still alive." The police vehicle drove up to an officer. There was a lengthy conversation. The policewoman came over to the car Charlie and Lerato were driving and didn't look too happy. Apparently, the retired detective had been badly beaten and was on his way to the hospital in a critical condition.

"Oh no, that's shocking," Charlie gasped. "I hope it had nothing to do with our visit earlier. What's going on here? Trying to run us off the road, beating up a retired detective…"

"We don't know yet what happened and why, madam," the police officer said. "A neighbour heard noises and screams coming from Mr. van Rooyen's house and called the sector vehicle. It's unlikely a domestic case. Mr. van Rooyen's wife died nine years ago and after his son moved out, he's been living alone. Damn bastards, doing this to an old man!"

"Is the victim conscious?" Lerato asked and got out of the car.

The officer walked over to her colleagues to inquire and they talked a while longer. He came back with a grim look on his face. "Lennart was not conscious when he was found. They stabilised him on the way to the hospital."

"Madam, please don't interfere with the police investigation. We don't want anybody else to get hurt. You should be careful. Please call us immediately if you feel threatened." The policeman on the scene said. "Or go back to Johannesburg."

"Thank you, officer. We are not here to interfere with anything. We are just collecting evidence, then we'll be on our way. Is there anybody else we could speak to about the case?" Lerato probed.

"You are talking about the Peele case?"

"Yes, the Peele case," Lerato confirmed.

"Lennart was working on that case with another detective. Carlos Oosthuizen. He was transferred to Cape Town beginning of the year."

That was not exactly good news.

"Thank you for your help, officer. We sincerely hope that Mr. van Rooyen makes a full recovery and you find those cowards."

The police officer nodded sombrely. "We take care of our own, madam."

Shortly after, Lerato and Charlie made their way back to the guest house in Humewood.

"Poor guy, this Lennart," Lerato said as they left the flashing lights behind.

"Even if he didn't tell us the whole truth, what did he do to deserve that?"

"Somebody with big bucks doesn't want us to dig deeper. That much is clear."

"The husband?" Charlie wondered.

"Could be." Lerato kept her eyes on the road.

"I'm beat. You never mentioned that we might be in mortal danger when you asked me to help you with this case."

"I'm so sorry, Charlie," Lerato glanced at her yawning friend. "I never meant to drag you into something like that. I had no idea. We must be close to the truth. The question is: how did this thug found out about us? What has he got to do with the case? If this Carlos Oosthuizen was transferred to Cape Town, I will find him and get some answers."

"Maybe you can talk to him over the phone when we are back in Joburg," Charlie yawned. "Enough travelling for a while. At least for my part…"

"We still have a meeting with Mr. Peele tomorrow. Then we can go home. I'll see what I need to do next. If I have to go down to Cape Town, you won't have to go with. Gee, I'm hungry. Where do we get something to eat?"

"I could give Mrs. Portwich a call and ask her to prepare something."

"Sure. I can't let this new case get out of hand. The honeymoon is barely three months away," Lerato mused. "…and things are already heating up."

They had dinner at the guest house, and luckily, Deepak Misra did not.

Chapter EIGHT

Robert Peele waited at a table for two in the front yard of a chic boutique restaurant on the Marine Parade. He was preparing to meet with an old college pal, who was on a visit to Port Elizabeth, and straight after with some businesswoman from Johannesburg.

Tourists and locals enjoyed a glorious morning by the ocean and the tables on the veranda upfront quickly filled with patrons. Good, the more people and noise that surrounded him, the more incognito the conversations would be.

There was something important that his friend needed to discuss that couldn't be spoken about over the phone. That's why he had come all the way from England to Port Elizabeth. Given the nature of their relationship, Robert Peele had an inkling what the discussion would be about. A debt was owed and needed to be paid.

The businessman had chosen a corner table to keep an eye on the comings and goings at the eatery. Much safer to meet here than at the office, where the walls had eyes and ears. A waiter brought him the water with lemon he had ordered and placed the menu on the white table cloth. He checked his watch. It was nearly 10 o'clock and Robert Peele felt hungry.

"Could you bring me the escargots in garlic butter, please? We'll order breakfast as soon as my friend arrives." Snails were not exactly a breakfast dish, but the waiter didn't flinch.

"Certainly, sir."

What could be keeping Deepak? They had shared a room at Cambridge and Robert Peele knew how punctual his former roommate was, to the point of being pedantic. It was just Deepak's personality and quite unlike the South African way where being late was acceptable if not expected.

Deepak Misra arrived as the businessman began to tuck into his garlicky snails.

"There you are," Robert Peele greeted him. "I was getting worried,"

"Sorry, I was on an important call." Deepak sat down. The waiter stood next to him a moment later, handing him a breakfast menu. "Thanks," the

Englishman grunted.

"Can I get you something to drink, sir?" The waiter asked politely.

"Yes, you can bring me a Sprite zero, please. Lemon, no ice. And… hang on, the same as my friend here."

"Certainly, sir." The waiter came back with the clear, bubbly cool drink, poured the liquid into a spotless glass and placed the escargot dish in front of him. "Would you like to hear today's specials?" he asked.

"Give us a minute here, will you?" Robert Peele said and the waiter left.

"I'm glad to see that their service is as good as last time we were here."

"Wouldn't dream of taking you to a place with lousy service, my man. Can't risk having you throttle the poor waiters," Robert Peele smirked.

"You still think I'm too finicky?"

"Never stopped thinking that." He switched the topic. "How's the family?"

"Good, good, Rob. And yourself?"

"Ah, I'll survive, I suppose. Have a new girlfriend now. Vanessa. You should meet her. She's a stunner and you won't believe…"

"You know that I look at these… things differently. No offence."

"None taken." Robert Peele lowered his voice. "So let's get down to the point. What brings you to our shores?"

"I'm getting married, Rob." Deepak Misra took a deep long swig of his beverage and suppressed a burp. "And I might need your help."

"You're getting what?" Robert Peele's jaw dropped. He pushed the small plate to the centre of the table. The six hollow shells were still shiny with melted butter.

"Married, Rob. Really nice chick, too. Family's originally from Goa but she grew up in Zurich. Beautiful and educated. Her brother Sanjay introduced us at a party in London. She's 32 and desperate to get married. The ideal wife for me."

"A trophy wife? But you are… certainly not the marrying type," Robert Peele said. He had benefitted nicely from the Misras' influence and knew when to bite his tongue.

The waiter came to take the empty plates from the table and scribbled down the breakfast order.

"Anything else I can get you?"

"We are good for now. Thank you," Robert Peele said and Deepak Misra waited until the man was out of earshot.

"I'm certainly not the marrying type, but my father won't take no for an answer anymore. He found out about Alec and is prepared to look the other way if... I get married and save the family honour," he groaned.

"How did he find out?"

"Some PI vermin, I suppose. Didn't exactly give him the third degree to find out. He was upset enough about Alec staying in a flat I'm paying for, so I didn't want him to dig deeper and have him on my case no end."

"Sure, I understand. So what are you going to do? Live with that - woman - happily ever after?"

"Well, she's quite traditional. She'll adapt."

Robert Peele snorted contemptuously.

"Not in that sense," Deepak Misra clarified. "Loves to wear modern clothes, makeup and all that and she's everything but stupid. Quite presentable actually. And isn't that the purpose? The alternative is that my father will cut me off and why would I want to risk that?"

"Hmm. It's your decision, my friend. What is it you wanted to discuss with me? Surely, you could have told me over the phone that you are getting married."

The waiter arrived with their breakfast and Deepak Misra waited until he was gone, before giving his old friend an answer.

"You guessed it. I need back up. Some kind of insurance. Just in case I can't talk sense into her," he said cryptically. "Before she turns into an unbearable ball and chain like… you know."

"You mean…?" Robert Peele didn't have to say the name. They both knew.

"Yes, that's what I mean. We'll be coming to South Africa for our honeymoon after the big, fat Indian wedding in Chennai in November." He rolled his eyes. "It will be like a Bollywood movie if my mother has her way. And she normally does."

"But Deepak," his friend objected. "If you want babies, you can't just off her. Plus, you are the one with all the connections. For which I'll be eternally grateful, by the way. So don't get me wrong, but what can I do for you that David cannot? "

"David was in a shootout with the police." Deepak

Misra said the word police so softly that Robert Peele had to guess as to what it was. "Dead. Replacement is hard to come by. My Dad's not happy, I can tell you. So that's why I need your help, Rob."

"Dead?"

Deepak Misra nodded his head and grimaced. "That's why I need a backup plan, a plan B. In case she flips out. That's a remote possibility."

"Holy shit, that's unfortunate about David, man. Didn't think a guy like him could slip up when it comes to the police. So what is it I can do?"

"You could organise something for me here on your side, Rob. In Cape Town, actually. That's where we'll honeymoon most of the time." He held up his hands. "Just as a backup solution. There are not that many assassins in my circles back home." Again, the word assassins was barely audible.

"Shit! Let me think around that. Bloody hell, Deepak you're getting me into trouble." Robert was sweating bullets. He cursed the day he'd accepted Deepak's offer to take care of his marital problems for him. "Don't even know where to start searching for someone like that. It's not that easy, you know."

"You owe me, Rob, remember?" Deepak Misra whispered as he stared coldly at his fidgeting friend. "Well, I need your help this time around and you'd better make a plan. That's all there is to it. And as I said at this stage it's only a plan B."

"Alright, alright. I'll see what I can do," Robert Peele kneaded his hands. "How long are you booked into the Humewood guesthouse?"

"Until Sunday. I also need you to check something else for me."

"What else?" Robert Peele whispered.

"There are two women at the guesthouse who seem to have their noses in my business. Perhaps my odious father organised a chaperone-service for his wayward son. Who knows? But I'd like to do my own thing, while I'm here. Saw them both at the airport in Johannesburg. We were on the same flight to PE and now they are staying at the same guesthouse. I mean what are the odds? If they are on my tail, I'll give your guy his first job. To test his talent, so to speak. They drive a rental car. Blue KIA."

"That doesn't leave me much time. Man, you've got my balls in a vice."

"You owe me, my friend." Deepak Misra smiled coolly. "…and it might not even come to that. Just in case they are getting in the way. We make a good team, don't we?"

Robert Peele nodded and put his fork down. "Got it: a blue KIA. Do you have their names and number plate?"

"They stay at the same guesthouse in Humewood. That's where you start. Clean forgot their names. Your guy will know how to find out. I'll be going out tonight. Sampling the local fare, so to speak." Deepak Misra grinned mischievously. "You're welcome to join me, but I don't think it's your kind of entertainment."

"Sorry old man, you're on your own with that sort of thing. If I can get hold of somebody suitable, I'll give you a call and we can meet."

"Suit yourself. Do we have a deal?" Their eyes locked for a brief moment.

"I'm just not sure I'm good at that sort of thing… but I'll give it a try."

"That's what I want, Rob. I scratch your back and you scratch mine. It's always been our agreement and that's all there is to it."

And if you don't play ball, my man, you'll be next, he thought to himself with utter disdain. Friendship only went so far, and a debt was a debt.

*

"What was the place called again?" Lerato asked Charlie for the umpteenth time. They were again on their way to the seafront. This time their destination was an eatery on the Marine Parade Robert Peele's secretary had suggested. Lerato had phoned him to make an appointment with a cock and bull story that she wanted to do business with him.

"Lerato! It's called Donatello's. You said it's a pizza place." Charlie studied her cell phone. It should come up on the right any moment now."

Lerato slowed down and turned into the parking lot. They had picked up the replacement car at the car hire place not far from there - a white Polo.

"Don't you think it's a bit odd that she didn't ask questions when you phoned yesterday?"

"Not really. I mean, as long as he thinks it's about business. Could it be that fancy schmantzy place over there? Sure enough, that's Donatello's." She pointed to a restaurant at the very end of a row of shops.

"Doesn't look like a pizza joint to me…"

"I don't have a good feeling about this, Lerato," Charlie said suddenly.

"What? You're telling me now? And you keep saying that you are not psychic."

"I'm not psychic."

"Okay then, here we are. Let's give it a shot. It's a public place and quite popular by the looks of it. What could possibly happen?"

"I'm not sure how to describe it. It's just a hunch."

Lerato Gwala found a parking spot not far from the restaurant's entrance. "Look, we should be fine. That's our goal for today. Number one, tick. The insurance company replaced the car without any hassles, and number two… we need to get some intel on this guy Peele. So let's make the best of it."

"What if he doesn't like the idea that it's a ruse to get him to speak to us? Can't your police friends back us up?"

"And what reason would I have for wasting their time like that? Stop panicking. We've already been chased by some moron. If he was behind it, we'll find out soon enough. But he doesn't strike me as a gangbanger. Not someone to get his hands dirty."

"Can you be sure? Somebody with so much money could have henchman to do the dirty work for him."

"I can't be sure about anything, Charlie. So are we going in or what?"

"Well, it's your call. I'm just tagging along. Just remember that I don't have a black belt in karate like you. Do you have your weapon?"

"Ready and loaded." Lerato Gwala lifted her jacket a little and revealed a holster with a gun in it. They walked towards the restaurant. The veranda was surrounded by a wooden fence and a few bougainvillaea plants were blooming pink in large blue pots. As a matter of habit, Lerato surveyed the outdoor area before they took the stairs to the veranda. A grim-looking man seemed to be waiting at a table in the back next to one of the plant pots.

"There, that must be Mr. Peele," she said before one of the waiters approached.

"Hope he's not too cross that we are late," Charlie said.

Lerato shrugged. "Well then… here goes nothing."

The man was on his cell phone and not in the best of moods as his search for a hitman was not proving very successful. Robert Peele hated the mere thought of it. How could he be sure that whatever happened would not be traced back to him? 'I'll phone you back...' He jumped up as he caught sight of them.

"Robert Peele," he introduced himself politely. "The one and only."

"Lerato Gwala." They shook hands.

"And you are...?" He looked at Charlie. There was no mention of two businesswomen, but she is pretty, he thought and his mood lifted.

"My name is Charlotte Proudfoot, Ms Gwala's business associate."

Lerato gave him a business-like smile that matched her business outfit.

"Allow me." The waiter pulled up an extra chair. "Anything to drink for the ladies?"

"Not right now, thank you," Charlie answered in a kind tone and the waiter disappeared. "I'm very sorry we are a bit late."

"Not to worry. Made good use of the time. How can I help you? You said something about wanting to discuss business?" Mr. Peele began on a confident note and put his cell phone on the table. "Who did you say told you about me?"

A group of women at one of the tables broke out in peals of laughter.

"A mutual acquaintance and yes, we are here about business." Lerato took out her license and held it out for Robert Peele to see. Although it wasn't necessary, she liked to bring her license along for situations like this one. He squinted at the card.

"We've learned about your wife's passing, and a client of mine has asked me to find out more about the circumstances of her death. I hope you don't mind my asking you a couple of questions."

Robert Peele stared at her and began to tremble. The last thing he had expected was a couple of PIs. Vermin, as Deepak called them. Not the women, Deepak had mentioned, because he'd seen them arrive in a white car. But troublesome enough. This day was not going well at all.

"Is this some kind of trick?" He sneered.

"No, no trick."

"Her family contacted you? That's rich of them! You see, my wife's death broke my heart. Such a senseless death and just for some jewellery. I'm trying to put the whole affair behind me. So, yes, I definitely do mind."

He was working himself up into a state and the two sleuths were shocked by his sudden rage. He had gone from zero to one hundred in a split second.

"Mr. Peele, that's not exactly why we are here, but I'm sure it is also in your own interest if the matter…" Lerato began, but he cut her off without much ado.

"I suggest you leave now. Tell her mother that they'll be hearing from my lawyers if she tries to pin this on me. Unbelievable!" Robert Peele stood up abruptly and chased the waiter away, who approached with pen and notepad, ready to take their order. "No man, we are leaving!" The baffled waiter fled back inside.

"But we are not working for your wife's mother."

"Oh, I'm glad to hear it. Her aunt, then? Old bitch has plenty of moollah. That's what you call doing business? Good day to you," Robert Peele barked at the two women. "And don't contact me again. Vermin!"

He took out his cell phone and waved it in front of Charlie's face. Startled, she took a step back and picked up her handbag.

"Very well then, Mr. Peele," Lerato said. "We won't bother you any longer."

The man just waved dismissively and tried to get hold of somebody on his cell phone. The two sleuths walked back to their rental car in a daze.

"Can you believe it? What an a**hole!" Charlie blustered. "Why would he think that his wife's family sent us to investigate him?"

"This guy has plenty to hide, that's for sure. Damn, he seemed quite civilised at first. And you still warned me as we walked in."

"Well, I just had a hunch."

"Damn, I should have listened to you. That'll teach me." Lerato wasn't at all pleased with the outcome of their brief meeting. "What a waste of time, and not a good thing that he knows our names now."

"With some luck, he's already forgotten them. In his mind, we are vermin. If he's that aggressive, we won't have much luck with his staff, either. So what are we going to do now?"

"Get out of here and quickly." Lerato started the engine. "We can go down to the beach for a walk to clear our heads and do more research on the internet later. All the things we never got a chance to do last night." They drove down the road, looking for parking. "I hope nobody is following us this time!"

Charlie turned around. "Nope, doesn't look like it."

"If Misra and Peele meet - and I'm sure they will - we should get us some photos as proof."

"Proof of what? We can already prove that Misra came to Port Elizabeth."

"It would be better to get them in a picture together. Hell, why is there so much traffic all of a sudden?" Lerato hooted at a tourist bus that cut her off.

"Must be the surfing event. International Surfing Championship. Didn't you see the posters along the road?" Charlie said.

"No, I didn't. Great, that means masses of tourists and every bed in town is booked. Good thing we won't be staying much longer."

"Who do you think he is phoning right now?" Charlie wondered. "I hope we didn't make a monumental mistake by meeting that ogre."

"Probably crapping out his secretary for not asking questions before making an appointment. Poor woman," Lerato sighed. "Look at all these people!"

"He might be phoning Mr. Misra to fill him in. Maybe we should skip the beach and have lunch somewhere. Boy, it's getting hot." Charlie pulled out a bottle of water and took a long swig. "Want some?" Lerato grabbed the bottle and sipped the water.

"I said I would listen to you, so I will." She passed the beach and drove along the Marine Parade toward the hotel mile. "Let's get lunch and brainstorm. If we just knew how to access their phone records… one needs a Section 205 from the court, but that's not so easy. There has to be a crime or probable cause," Lerato said. "So no chance of that. But I had an even better idea." She grinned and took out a small device.

"Oh? What's that?" Charlie asked surprised.

"I slipped a tracking device into Mr. Peele's suit pocket when he got all worked up. He never noticed a thing. Now, all we have to do is track him. We'll have lunch, brainstorm, wait… whatever. Either they meet or we leave town."

Lerato parked in a hotel parking lot.

"You sly vermin! I never noticed a thing, either!" Charlie slapped Lerato's arm.

"Hey, I'm driving! Yeah, I admit it was a pretty

good idea."

"So, what does your tracker tell you now?"

"That Mr. Peele is on the move. He's coming our way," Lerato said and looked at Charlie in surprise. "Probably just driving past."

"What? What if he sees us?" Charlie hissed.

"He won't." Lerato had parked next to a double-cab bakkie that obscured the view from the road. "Look, there are oodles of white cars around and plenty of shoppers and tourists. And look what I brought." She reached behind her seat and pulled a button-down overdress, a dust cloth and a hat out of a plastic bag.

"What's all that for?" A wide-eyed Charlie wanted to know.

"Easy. We'll change our look. This one is for you and I'll put on that one and the hat. Whatever Peele does, he won't know me from the next black person. He never looked at me properly. So I could be one of the cleaners for all he cares and you are some slapper waiting for her boyfriend or something."

"Slapper, hey?!"

"Or tourist… works like a charm."

"I'm impressed Ms Gwala," Charlie said. "Very impressed."

"Good. Here, put that on." Lerato gave her a pair of jeans and a t-shirt. "And tie up your hair. You'll look like a different person. Watch and learn. We'll simply wait until he's at his destination, then we'll swoop in and take pictures. Easy."

"You are a genius!" Their hopeless situation had just turned around. "What if he goes back to his office?"

Lerato shrugged.

"We'll just hang around and see who he's meeting. At the very least we give it a try." She put on the plain overdress in the cover of the bakkie and became indistinguishable from so many cleaners one could find everywhere.

"Let's see where he's going now." Lerato studied her device, while Charlie struggled into the t-shirt and jeans on the passenger seat.

"There you are, you naughty man… just behind us?!" Lerato slid down in her seat and motioned for Charlie to do the same. She turned a little and saw Robert Peele striding past behind their car and toward the entrance to the hotel. "Damn this device is good!"

"What is it?" Charlie sat stock-still, trying not to draw attention to herself.

"Our guy is here in the parking lot!" Lerato hissed.

Before he went through the glass doors, Mr. Peele turned around and scanned the parked cars, obviously looking for someone. Charlie looked away and when she looked again, he had disappeared inside.

"Oh, my word!" Lerato sat up straight in the driver seat and took a deep breath. "Bingo! He didn't waste any time."

Nobody had paid the slightest attention to them, but they didn't know who Robert Peele had been looking for. They got out of the car, greeted the parking guard and walked into the hotel lobby. Groups of chatting surfers were standing around everywhere. It was obvious that they had arrived for their international event.

"Not a bad place to be right now," Lerato grinned. "There he is." She turned around quickly and began to dust around one of the flowerpots, while Charlie sat down on one of the comfortable armchairs placed around a low glass table and picked up a newspaper. Robert Peele was waiting by himself in front of the hotel restaurant.

"Let's see if he's going into the restaurant."

"Okay."

"We should split up. I stick with our mark, and you can sit here in the hotel lobby and read magazines or go to the car when you get bored." Lerato dropped the keys into Charlie's lap and began to work every dust-able surface around. "Wonder if he's meeting with our chap Misra," she whispered close to her friend's ear.

"Speak of the devil!" Charlie said in a soft voice and hid behind the newspaper she was holding up. They nodded subtly to each other when Deepak Misra made an appearance. He rushed to the back of the lobby, apparently to meet his friend.

Lerato dusted the artwork behind the armchair as the men went inside the restaurant where Robert Peele had, as he often did, reserved a corner table. Only one other table was occupied. Lerato made her way leisurely toward the restaurant and played around with her cell phone, softly speaking in Xhosa with an imaginary caller. She was virtually invisible to the people she was snapping pictures of.

The fake cleaning lady heard bits and pieces of the

conversation, making herself useful with the dust cloth not far from the corner where the two men had their meeting.

Soon, Lerato had to move to another part of the restaurant in order to avoid suspicion, but she'd heard that Robert Peele told his friend about the odd meeting he'd had with two female PIs, who were asking questions about his wife's murder. Not to worry, he'd sent them packing at once.

"It must be the same women from the guesthouse," Deepak Misra said.

Lerato grinned to herself. If you just knew, she thought and took another picture for good measure.

Then something unexpected happened: to her surprise, a third man joined them.

Can this get any better? She recorded what was being said. Deepak Misra was apparently in the market for a hitman! Her blood ran cold when she realised that she and Charlie might become the hitman's first mark.

The men quickly lost interest in talking about the female PIs for some reason, she could not clearly understand. They continued talking about some kind of backup plan in Cape Town.

Cape Town! It was the honeymoon destination of the newlywed Misra couple. She rubbed a spot on the floor under an adjoining table behind a wall divider and nodded to an imaginary colleague outside, trying to draw as little attention to herself as possible.

The waiters didn't look twice at the cleaner crouching on the floor and all the while, her phone was recording the meeting. It didn't take long for the suspected hitman to say goodbye and that he'd be in touch.

"What are you doing there?" One of the waiters asked her in Xhosa. Lerato jumped. "I dropped something."

"If you must clean now, dust the sideboard over there."

"Sure, no problem," she said and got to work, relieved that her disguise had worked even on him.

After a seafood platter, two cocktails and very little talk, Deepak Misra and Robert Peele made ready to leave the restaurant. Lerato Gwala had her pictures and a recorded conversation to boot. Now there was just one more thing to do.

She grabbed a mop that was leaning against the wall between the toilets in the passage next to the restaurant, skilfully blocked the way and grabbed the tracker from Robert Peele's suit pocket as the men left.

"Sorry, master, sorry," she mumbled and looked down. She made sure that her face remained hidden by her hat, in case one of the men gave her a closer look. But not even Deepak Misra bothered and the button-sized tracker ended up safely in her pocket.

Unfortunately, she dropped her cell phone into the water bucket a minute later, as she put the mop back.

"Shit!" She fished for the phone in the dirty water. "Shit, shit, shit! That's all I need!" She cursed and pushed the door to the ladies room open. In one of the cubicles, she wiped the phone furiously with toilet paper and took off her cleaner's outfit and left through the front door the way she had come in.

Charlie had gone back to the car by now and was waiting for her friend.

"Where have you been?" Charlie asked when she finally spotted Lerato. "Those guys left ages ago."

"Promise you won't laugh!" Lerato muttered and took off her floppy hat.

"What?"

"Promise you won't laugh!" Lerato repeated with a

stern expression.

"Okay, I won't laugh."

Lerato locked the car doors. "I recorded a conversation between our two guys and another guy. He came in through the back and I think he was a hitman."

"But… that's great! What's so funny about that?" Charlie looked confused. She had taken off her disguise as well, and her auburn hair was once again loose.

"Well, we might not be able to use the recording because I dropped my phone in a bucket with dirty water."

"You did what'?" Charlie was more surprised than amused. "How did that happen?" Lerato scoffed.

"I was a cleaner, remember? When those guys left, I retrieved the tracking device. Successfully, by the way. They didn't look at me once, but then, I don't know how it happened… I dropped my phone and it landed in that disgusting bucket."

"Shit." Charlie was horrified.

"That's what I said. I'm so angry with myself. We might have lost the recording. It wouldn't be admissible in court anyway but now we can't even play it back for my client. And the pictures I took…"

"They might also be lost?"

"Yes."

"Damn. Wait. I'll speak to Jono. If anybody knows how to save your data, it's him."

Lerato sighed. "Oh please, speak to him! At least I heard some interesting stuff."

She told Charlie what she had witnessed in the restaurant.

"Wow. That's heavy. If Deepak Misra already knows why we are in town, perhaps we should take the next flight out. I don't want to risk a run-in with his henchman. The guy who tried to run us off the road is still giving me the creeps."

"Maybe it's the same guy," Lerato said.

"Could be. Looks like we are swimming with sharks here. Not that I'd mind doing that in a touristy way."

"Another time maybe," Lerato said and winked, then caught herself. "We shouldn't joke about stuff like that. I don't want to become shark food!"

"In the past two days, I think we got more than we bargained for," Lerato moaned. "Let's get home as soon as possible without attracting attention." She handed her phone to Charlie.

"Yuck." Charlie gingerly picked the phone up with

a tissue. "It's not working, remember? I'll have to use my phone."

"Damn!"

"I'll make the flight reservations and Jono can pick us up from the Gautrain station in Rosebank. The sooner we can get back to Joburg, the better."

"What does your intuition say? Are we going to survive this trip?"

"Hey, I'm not a circus attraction that goes into a trance on command."

"Then we'll just have to take our chances, I guess."

"You're guessing right." Charlie held up her hand to ask her friend for silence. While Lerato Gwala was steering the car, she made the online reservations, then dialled her landline in Johannesburg.

Jono answered the phone straight away.

'I've been waiting for you to call!' Jono said in an accusing tone. "You didn't answer your phone yesterday. Is everything okay with you?'

'I was kind of busy. Sorry for not phoning, we literally fell into bed last night. How are the doggies doing?'

'Our dear neighbour raised hell again in the street in the morning. This time with somebody else's dog.'

'For goodness sake, I wonder why she can't just put her dogs on a leash!'

'I know. So what's been going on in Port Elizabeth?'

'Too much to tell you over the phone. We're coming back tomorrow morning on the next flight. Can you fetch us from the Gautrain station in Rosebank? I'll let you know when we arrive.'

"The plane lands at 11:07," Lerato reminded her in the background.

'The plane lands at 11:07 at OR Tambo, so we should be in Rosebank at around 12:00.'

'Okay sure, no problem. So you're still determined to carry on with the case?'

'Yeah, well, I had my doubts for a while, but it's too important.'

'Sounds ominous. You sure you're okay?'

'I'll tell you everything tomorrow.'

'Mom and Dad will not be very happy if I tell them what you're up to.'

'You won't dare tell them.'

'I might just.'

'No, you won't. I know you too well. Let me handle that.'

'Okay then, we'll speak tomorrow. I'll be in Rosebank at 12.'

'Thank you, you're my favourite brother. We need you to do something for us, but we'll speak tomorrow.'

'Okay... anything for you. Take care.' They hung up.

"The dogs are alright. Jono says the neighbour's dogs picked a fight with some other dog," Charlie groaned. "Will these people never learn?"

"You and your neighbour issues," Lerato chuckled. "Phone the SPCA or the police if this keeps happening. Listen, we should get some takeaways. No way am I going to take the risk of meeting our British friend over dinner."

"As long as we make it to the airport in one piece, I'm happy," Charlie sighed.

"We are booked in for another two days. That should throw him off our scent."

They returned to the guesthouse with Chinese takeaway food in the afternoon. Low carb for Charlie. As they approached their room, Lerato motioned for Charlie to stay back and drew her gun.

"What?" Charlie mouthed, but Lerato just pointed

to their room.

They heard a noise in the room. Then another.

Charlie had never seen Lerato move so fast. It took her only a moment to open the door and point her weapon. Charlie stuck her head around the corner and had to laugh.

On the floor sat a fat ginger cat, licking leftovers they had discarded in the bin. It was soon established that the cat had seemingly jumped in through a small window above the shower and made itself at home, knocking over the bin in the process.

The cat stared at the two women, ducked and made its way out of the door between Lerato's legs.

"Damn…" Lerato put her gun away.

"You can say that again."

"That could have easily been our friend from the hotel."

"Time to go home, Ms Gwala." Charlie sat down on her bed and tidied up the mess the cat had left behind.

"Yes, time to go home," the courageous PI agreed.

Chapter NINE

Meanwhile, at the mansion on the hill, the butler opened the door for a man in a dark business suit. He formally guided him past a dining table that could easily seat twenty-four guests. They walked through a vast living area with a marble fireplace straight to the west-facing veranda.

The visitor marvelled at the way the fireplace seemed to grow out of the polished marble floors. A small fire crackled in the opening. The artwork at the mansion was exquisite and must have cost a fortune. Bought with the money Robert Peele had made from shady business deals, the guest was only too aware of.

The butler made himself scarce as soon as the guest had been securely delivered to the beautiful outdoor space.

Vanessa January, Peele's girlfriend was already there. The beautiful woman sat on a large outdoor sofa, clad in a skimpy see-through garment, her arm outstretched over the backrest, sipping white wine.

She lifted her glass in greeting. What she lacked in upbringing was made up by genuine beauty and she was well aware of it.

"There you are, Brian! Glad you could make it. John is not with you?" Robert Peele greeted the man.

"He's otherwise engaged," Brian apologised. He knew that John D'Abreu lay on the stained carpet in his flat in town, his hands tied behind his back, a cloth gag in his mouth and a bullet wound between his eyes. The well-known drug dealer had done an unauthorised deal behind the big boss's back and Brian had been sent in to clean up.

"Ah well, he doesn't know what he's missing," Robert Peele gave a short laugh.

"No, he doesn't," Brian said and walked up to the balustrade of the glass-encased veranda. "What a wonderful sunset." His smile didn't reach his eyes.

"If it was summer, we'd all be sitting in the infinity pool, sipping cocktails with a horde of marvellous women. Smooth jazz and the whooshing of the surf in the background. John just loves coming here."

"I'm sure, he does. You have an amazing home up here, Mr. Peele." He turned around to face his host, who gestured with his usual Gin & Tonic in hand.

"Well, thank you, Brian. I must say I enjoy it tremendously. And do call me Robert. We're all friends here, are we not?"

Beautiful Vanessa glanced at the guest for a fleeting second, smiled knowingly and stopped swinging her leg forth and back.

"We sure are, Robert. Could I please have something to drink?" One corner of his mouth was slightly drawn up in disdain. It was the only sign in his stern face that he did not quite approve of his host.

"Where are my manners?" Robert Peele said and snapped his fingers at Vanessa. "Do you mind darling? Pour us a drink, will you?"

"Of course, love, anything for you," Vanessa January got up and brushed Robert Peele's neck with her well-formed lips. The gown she was wearing seemed to reveal more of her rounded figure than hiding it, and the guest had certainly noticed.

"What can we offer you, Brian?" She asked languidly.

"Do you have Scotch on the rocks?"

"Scotch we do have," she replied. "Any particular Scotch?"

"You choose," Brian said and sat down on a white wicker chair with a high fan-shaped back. He sat on the front edge of the seat as if the chair with its large cushions was uncomfortable.

"Very well. Anything for you, darling?" The seductive woman asked.

"I'll have another one of these babies." Robert Peele held up his tumbler.

His girlfriend knew his favourite drink. A double gin and tonic with ice and a slice of lemon. "Coming up," she said and turned around to the sideboard to prepare the drinks. Ice cubes clattered into the glasses.

"So, Brian, we have something to celebrate, don't we?"

"We do, Robert and I must say it is a mutually beneficial deal. John was very pleased with the… favourable conditions." What Brian didn't say was that John hadn't lived long enough to enjoy the proceeds of their mutually beneficial deal.

"Good, good. I'm glad to hear it."

Vanessa held a small sachet in the palm of her hand that Brian had dropped in her lap as he'd walked past the sofa. She tore off one end and trickled the fine powder into her boyfriend's glass. It was a rather special powder. Invisible to the eye, tasteless to the tongue and virtually undetectable after ingestion. He wouldn't die, of course, just end up very intoxicated – for now. That was important. Vanessa January put all her hatred for the man who subjected her to demeaning kinky sex games and a slew of other lovers whenever he was in town, into the act of adding the poison to Robert Peele's drink.

Pleased that her assignment was finally coming to an end, she carefully whisked the contents of the glass, then slipped the sachet and stirrer inside a serviette, taking care not to stain the counter.

She replaced the stirrer with a new one, wiped her hands clean and turned around, nodding imperceptibly to the guest. They knew how to pull off this game and had done it scores of times before.

"There you go, Brian. Scotch on the rocks." She turned to Robert Peele and held out the tumbler with the double gin and tonic. "Here darling, there's your G & T. Give me the other glass. Enjoy." Robert Peele handed his girlfriend the near-empty tumbler and gave her a little slap on the plump behind.

"Thank you, Vanessa. Are you not going to have

another white wine?"

"I still have, Robbie," she said in a silky voice and put the glass on the counter.

"Suit yourself, darling." He turned to admire the sunset. It was glorious. A palette of vivid orange and red, painting the sky and the glistening ocean surface. It was the last sunset he should ever see.

The guest genuinely appreciated sunsets and beautiful views as well.

He appreciated anything beautiful and couldn't help but sneak a glance at Vanessa's stunning curves. Not long after the poison had taken effect, two people on the veranda were on top of each other, pumping wildly. It was their ritual when an assignment was coming to an end. Victory sex, so to speak. The sofa had witnessed a fair number of compromising situations, just that this time Robert Peele was not the one participating.

The flimsy gown lay in a heap on the floor and later ended up in the fireplace.

The rest of the evidence was stashed in one of the guest's suit pockets. Vanessa and her accomplice stood watching as the fabric burned to a crisp. She hated to see the silky gown destroyed, but it was safer this way, in case there were traces of the poison on it.

"Everything is ready," she whispered and slipped into another similar gown.

The butler would never know the difference between her gowns and he had seen many. All they had to do was to complete their assignment.

Vanessa and Brian staged the scene in such a way that more gin ended up in Robert Peele's stomach. Vanessa January waited for the sign, then screamed piercingly and Brian shouted. "Robert, Robert, you silly man, what are you doing? Come down from there!"

When Robert Peele slid over the balustrade owing to a firm push courtesy of Brian's gloved hands, a loud prolonged scream escaped not his lips but those of his scheming guest. "Aaaaahhhhh!!"

The victim of the ghastly setup bounced from rock to rock. His first encounter with the rocks below resulted in a crushed skull, as the coroner would note two hours later. The impacts that followed broke his neck, both his legs and his right shoulder before landing on the gravel close to the water's edge.

He also recorded that the victim had been alive

before the broken skull led to his instant death.

Robert Peele's butler came running from the kitchen, where he had been chatting to the cook and the maid. There was nothing they could do but stare down the depths, seeing very little in the fast-approaching darkness.

When it was over, the maid tried to console a hysterically sobbing Vanessa, making her drink a glass of warm sugar water, while the butler called the police. Soon police officers swarmed the place where Robert Peele had met his maker, taking statements and searching for evidence of possible wrong-doing.

In the confusion, Brian had made his getaway as planned. He'd found the passage, thundered down the stairs and ducked through the small door that had been left open. Twenty minutes later, he left the second-hand car with fake number plates in the parking lot on the other side of town and proceeded to his hiding place as planned.

The following morning, police found the abandoned vehicle, but alas no fingerprints or any evidence that could lead them to the mysterious guest. Once again, the clean-up had been successful and the big boss should be pleased.

Meanwhile, police investigations were taking place at the mansion.

"So, your boyfriend, Mr. Robert Peele, was drunk when he fell to his death?"

"I told you, he could get a bit… daring… whenever he had too much to drink. And for some reason, he had one Gin & Tonic after the other last night. Stress probably. He then climbed on the footstool over there and was over the balustrade before we could do anything to stop him."

"You were not alone out here, were you?"

"No, as I said before, he had invited somebody called Brian… Something and we had drinks outside."

"Were you planning to have dinner?"

"Not really… Robbie liked to play… games when certain guests were here. Not always but when he felt inclined." Vanessa Peele whispered the last sentence. The police officer checked her notes.

"We know. The butler, Luphelo Radebe, also known as Mr. Lupo, has already put us in the picture about the somewhat unusual parties that Mr. Peele sometimes organised, and that he had balanced on the balustrade before. So what happened last night?"

"It's rather embarrassing, but… Robbie expected me to play my part when he threw a party like that. Last night was about a business deal. It's not the first time he'd gotten drunk and climbed on the balustrade to show off. But he's never lost his footing before," Vanessa January bawled.

The policewoman nodded. The butler had already given a statement. He'd confirmed that he had not been present, but there had been no fight as far as he was aware, just chatting and laughter and drinking as usual. Mr. Peele had had drinks before the guests arrived, but he couldn't say how many.

"How long have you known Mr. Peele?"

"Oh, I met him at a Christmas Party at a hotel on the Marine Parade last year."

"What's the name of the hotel? And who was at the party?"

"I don't remember exactly. A girlfriend took me with her."

"We will need the name of the girlfriend and her contact details. Did Mr. Peele have family?"

"Not to my knowledge," Vanessa said. "He told

me that he is…was… an only child and that his parents passed away many years ago. Health issues. His wife Sarah died three years ago in a robbery here at the mansion. I'm not aware of any other family on his side." She snivelled into her tissue.

"I see. And you were here at the mansion yesterday?"

"I went out in the afternoon on an errand for about an hour or so. Then I spent the evening at the house, doing this and that until Robbie came home."

"Can anybody confirm this?" The policewoman searched Vanessa's face for any sign of twitching, but she had been dabbing her eyes with the tissue a lot.

"I suppose Mr. Lupo and the rest of the staff could," she suggested.

"Where did you go when you went out?"

"Shopping. Why is that important? My boyfriend, Mr. Peele, got drunk, clambered over the balustrade, which was no easy feat, and fell to his death."

"Have you met Mr. Peele's guest before?"

"No, I can't say that I have. This Brian Whoever wasn't at the party where I met Robbie and he didn't do anything wrong last night." Her tears began to flow again. The officer, who was taking fingerprints at the balustrade, rolled his eyes at the policewoman and handed her a box of tissues from the table.

"Right. So, where is this Brian Something now?"

Vanessa looked around. She seemed confused. "I don't know. Isn't he here somewhere?"

"No, he seems to have disappeared. You wouldn't know where this Brian might be found? We would like to question him."

"How am I supposed to know where he is? I was in shock and didn't keep tabs on him," Vanessa snarled. "I'm sorry... I didn't mean..."

"Madam, I'm just doing my job. Can you describe this guest for me?"

"Oh, you know, he was wearing a dark suit and he had short dark hair and you know... medium height. He didn't exactly stand out."

"The butler told us that he was wearing a Rolex watch," the policewoman baited her, reading from her notes. "And a golden ring on his right ring finger. Can you confirm that?"

"I didn't notice. Virtually all businessmen who come here, wear jewellery."

"What sort of business deal was discussed?"

"I have no idea."

"You must have some idea what this visitor wanted."

"I didn't really know Robbie's friends or guests. I just did what I was told when he… when he had a party out here. Maybe this Brian is well-known and doesn't want to be connected to… to… this." Vanessa January started crying again rather convincingly. "Oh Robbie, Robbie you can't just leave me here!"

The policewoman turned away in disgust and rolled her eyes. She silently cursed rich people who didn't know what to do with their time other than having scandalous parties.

"Andile, over to you," the police officer said to her colleague from the Crime Scene Investigating unit.

"Could you please come with me, Madam, so we can take your fingerprints," the junior CSI said to Vanessa.

"Why do you need to take my fingerprints? Are you accusing me of something?" It came out more aggressively than she had intended, but she couldn't wait to get out of this gilded prison.

"It's simply procedure, Madam. Should this be ruled as a crime scene, we must be able to exclude your fingerprints."

"Yes, yes of course." She slid out of her chair and followed the young man to the adjoining room, hips swaying.

"Madam, if you could please put on some clothes," the policewoman said firmly.

Vanessa turned around and grimaced. "Very well, I'll only be a moment." She went to her luxurious bedroom and closed the door in front of the young CSI.

"If you don't mind, officer."

He sighed and waited politely for 10 minutes before knocking on the door. "Madam… Madam…" Goodness, how long does it take her to put some clothes on? He thought before pressing down the door handle. It took him a split-second to realise that the room was empty.

The flimsy gown lay crumpled on the bedspread. She must be in the on-suite bathroom, he thought. But she wasn't in the bathroom. Andile made sure that there was nobody in the rooms next-door or on the large balcony either before he raised the alarm. Robert Peele's girlfriend had disappeared.

As always, Brian, whose real name was Hendrik

Grobelaar, had done his job and Vanessa January, whose real name was Glenda Kiewiet, had vanished into obscurity once more.

Now unemployed, Mr. Lupo quietly packed his belongings into the brown Nissan that was parked in the underground garage. The car was now clean and polished and virtually unrecognisable from the dirty rattle trap that had chased the two private investigators down the coastal road.

He made his way downhill to the township and his mother's house, where he would be applying for a new position, once the scandal about Mr. Peele's death had blown over. His deceased employer had had many business partners throughout the country and Mr. Lupo had kept their details carefully scribbled down in his notebook.

Apart from the impeccable skills required for his profession, the butler was well-acquainted with the whims of the rich and shameless and he knew how to keep his mouth shut.

*

'What? Andy, how could this happen?' Lerato Gwala was stunned. 'Yes, we saw him that morning and later at the hotel.'

Her business partner had just informed her that Robert Peele, the man, who'd very likely had a hand in his wife's killing, was dead. He was their only lead in the presumed murder plot against Deepak Misra's future wife and now he was dead.

Fallen to his death in a drunken daredevil stunt after climbing on the balustrade of the veranda at his lavish mansion.

The two people, who'd been with him at the time, had disappeared without a trace. And so had his butler, who was not even a suspect.

Lerato couldn't believe it. When her partner Andy Malherbe phoned, they had been working on the case at Charlie's house in Blairgowrie under the watchful eyes of two little dogs. Billie and Popcorn had found comfortable spots by the coffee table that was littered with papers and photographs.

Charlie stared at her with a shocked expression.

'I can't believe it hasn't even made the national news. Bloody hell! It could have been our British friend from Reading. Seems like there's trouble wherever he goes.'

"When did this happen?" Charlie whispered.

'Hang on a second, Andy,' Lerato said and pressed the phone against her chest. "The night we left," she told Charlie. "Apparently, Robert Peele fell to his death on the rocks from the veranda on the top floor of his mansion after having a drink with his girlfriend and a male guest.

The police are stumped, because if it was an accident, why did those people go into hiding? And if not, it raises a lot of questions. They put out a BOLO for the guy, but nothing yet. Andy thinks this could lead to a reopening of the case three years back." Charlie nodded.

She spoke into her cell phone again. 'Sorry Andy, Charlie just wanted to know when it happened. Do you want to send me the details? Okay. Thanks. How is Lennart doing? Aha, okay. I'm sorry to hear that. Yes. No, I'll leave in about an hour. Okay, see you then.'

"So?" Charlie wanted to know and Billie and Popcorn looked up.

"Lennart is still in a coma. Swelling on the brain, Andy said. They've arrested two guys, but nothing else."

"That's not good."

Charlie sighed and closed her laptop.

"Well, what can you do? We can't get involved in that case as well. Should we take a break? I think I need some coffee after this. Where are our pizzas?"

"Don't know, but I'm ready to finish up for today. Jono is still busy working on your phone. He says that most of the data was on the external SIM card."

"Like I know what that means…"

"It's storage space."

"Right. So are we getting the pictures I took in PE?"

"Give me a chance here."

A motorcycle sputtered outside, then hooted.

"That must be our pizza delivery. About time too, I'm starving," Lerato groaned and walked outside.

Chapter TEN

"O mere dilé haré hare gano chaló balié…" The romantic movie soundtrack played a little too loud for Deepak Misra's liking.

As much as he hated this charade, he danced with his smiling bride in the splendidly decorated ballroom fit for a Maharaja's wedding. Deepak was not in a festive mood and forced himself to smile as they were replaying the love scene in a well-known Hindi movie. The photographer clicked away.

It had been Maribel's choice for their first dance as a married couple. As was customary, the wedding party joined in and performed several group dances, while he dreaded what lay ahead.

A bridegroom, who was so inclined, could probably not wait to ravish his beautiful bride. The suite on top of the building with a magnificent view of the city was ideal for that. No expense had been spared and his mother had gone the whole hog. All Deepak could do was play along.

His smile was plastered to his face and his muscles started to cramp, but he had no choice, the festivities had to be endured.

Yet Deepak could not fault his bride. Her glossy hair was done up beautifully in an intricate hairdo, the veil attached to the top of her head, so that it wasn't in the way when they had to pose for the photographer. Smiling, smiling, keep smiling! He had to remind himself.

All the events his mother had painstakingly arranged didn't fill him with the expected joy and he wanted to slap some of those half-drunk, laughing faces, who kept congratulating him. The pressure had become so unbearable that he'd gone outside on a couple of occasions today.

November in Chennai was much more pleasant than autumn in England and he wished that his boyfriend could be with him. Instead, he phoned Alec in London while taking a walk in the hotel garden. He needed to get away from this wedding, take a few deep breaths to calm his nerves and keep his sanity.

Deepak drank very little alcohol that was served that day, but he would have loved to get stone drunk and skip right to the end of the damned event in a drunken stupor. It wasn't good enough to just get married and be done with it. No, you had to celebrate for a full three days and by now he was at the end of his tether.

True, his father could afford the most lavish of weddings and one had to outdo the last family wedding. As if it was an unwritten rule in the book of life. There was no reasoning with his parents, so Deepak didn't even try.

His mother had thrown herself into the preparations as if her life depended on it, and Maribel's mother had been delegated to organising the transport of Swiss and English relatives and some family members from Goa, all to be charged to his father's account. Mrs. Misra didn't have much to do, now that her children were grown, except to look after her husband and help raise her grandchildren.

Ashwin took care of his occasional needs outside the marriage bed in the big house. She knew that many men did so and accepted it stoically.

"I wonder what Mrs. Sharma is telling Auntie Sushila. They have been talking and laughing for a long time now." Mrs. Misra tried to catch a glimpse of the lively conversation her aunt was having with the mother of the bride.

Her husband patted her substantial thigh. "I don't believe they are talking about state secrets, love. Ah, look who's coming our way. Cousin Ubhay and his daughter… she's developed into a little beauty, hasn't she?" Ashwin Misra knew from experience that his wife was easily distracted in this way and it was a good thing, too. He scanned the ballroom for his son Deepak. Ah, there he was!

The bridegroom had just come back inside from the outdoor area and caught sight of his father who looked sternly at him. Everything had been done exactly as tradition demanded for a Vivaha.

The henna ceremony the day before the wedding, then on the first day, the Ganesh Pooja at the home of Deepak's uncle once removed with only the bridal party and relatives in attendance.

And now they had at last reached day three with the main 7-step Saptapadi ceremony, the cocktail hour and the reception. All the wedding guests were wearing the finest silks and brocades, himself included. The brocade scratched under his armpits and the turban felt heavy. Heavy like the burden he was carrying for the honour of the family.

Mr. Misra, who had forked out a small fortune for the festivities in the city's premier wedding venue, felt a tug on his brocaded sleeve. "Wonderful wedding, Ashwin." Yet another distant cousin who had come all the way from Delhi lifted his glass in passing while making a few dance moves. "Are we going to see the young people performing some more for us?"

"I sure hope so, Patil. Give them a chance to eat, drink and be merry!" The cousin joined another group of relatives.

"What a pratt," Ashwin Misra said bitterly to his cousin Pravin. "Still owes me money for the land he bought on the coast three years ago. He hasn't even finished building the house on it yet." He smiled at the guests who cared to look his way. They were impressed with the festivities, that much was clear. And that's what was important.

"Ashwin, don't be in a mood. It's your son's wedding. You should be full of joy that he finally got hitched," his cousin said.

"For sure, for sure, Pravin…"

Deepak Misra's eyes met his father's across the hall and the joy he had been feeling died immediately. The older man wasn't easily fooled.

Deepak had fled to the men's room after yet another romantic song and dance with his bride had ended. His new bride had already begun to feel like a ball and chain and he needed to exhale. He made sure that nobody was in the bathroom, before pressing the WhatsApp video call button. Thank goodness they had excellent Wi-Fi reception at this high-end venue.

'I don't know if I can take any more of this,' Deepak Misra whispered to Alec's miniature image. 'We're still to celebrate the civil marriage in London with all our friends and family who couldn't be here in India. Then it's off to the honeymoon in Cape Town. For TWO weeks. I want to scream!'

'Don't say, you haven't been warned.' Alec grinned cruelly.

'Got to go, love. Miss you terribly,' Deepak said in a whisper. 'Someone's coming.' Alec's image disappeared.

He adjusted his turban, stuck his tongue out at the

unhappy face in the mirror then pushed past the man, he was remotely related to.

"Damn business deals!" Deepak said to the man, who'd walked in. "Can't even enjoy my own wedding in peace."

The man was too drunk to care. Deepak had been on the video call for only 3 minutes, but as the groom, he couldn't be away for too long. Maribel and everybody else might become suspicious. He took a deep breath and went back to the resplendent ballroom, smiling all the way and acting happy.

There was still more formation dancing planned with more love-declarations from husband and wife and he dared not miss that. What a damn farce, Deepak thought bitterly and sighed.

She had worn a red wedding sari with gold embroidery, a silvery gown and now another dazzling sari in a jade colour - with matching shoes for each occasion, of course. Poor girl, I wonder if she's as unhappy as I am, he thought to himself. He looked at his bride and all he saw was happiness and the anticipation of a fulfilling wedding night.

*

Back in England, the civil wedding was done and dusted a week after the lavish affair in Chennai. Deepak had seen Alec for a stolen hour of passion here and there whenever he could get away from the breakfasts, lunches and dinners. And from his bride.

His other lover was away on holiday and had ordered him to be on standby in a month's time. Deepak wasn't so sure that he could wait that long. Surely, he would find some relief in Cape Town…

Since the civil ceremony, Maribel seemed to look forward to their trip to South Africa and had been shopping up a storm on his credit card in Southall with her cousins and her married sister.

Deepak didn't object. The longer he could keep her distracted the better. He had told Maribel that even if they moved into one of the cottages on his parents' property in Reading, she would be free to work at her pleasure.

The more she was occupied with such matters, the more time he had to pursue his own interests. It was meant to soften the blow that there would be no sexual relations between the two of them for the time being. Not if he could help it. But there was the little matter of producing the obligatory offspring. Well, they would cross that bridge when they got to it.

They had already discussed his issue during their wedding night in Chennai.

'I don't think I can do it,' he'd said and thrown himself down on the silky pillow next to his eager bride. She gave him a look of compassion. 'And here I thought you were just being the perfect gentleman.'

'And now you've changed your mind?'

'Look, there is no shame in being impotent. There are treatments for that sort of thing, you know.'

How understanding she had been. They had briefly spoken and Maribel had convinced herself that the problem was indeed a case of impotence and nothing else.

'Let me be a gentleman and sleep on the couch next door.'

'That's not necessary. We can sleep in the same bed. You are my husband now. Why would I mind? It's not nice to sleep all alone on your wedding night.'

'Look, darling, I feel embarrassed and would prefer not to sleep next to you – confronted with what I'm missing.'

'You must not be so negative, Deepak. If we are to

live together for the rest of our lives, we must learn to handle such issues sooner rather than later.'

'I know and I'm sorry. Just humour me tonight.'

'Very well. If that's what you want,' she'd sighed.

It had been a relief and he was confident that she could be trained in time. He'd left the bedroom in their wedding suite to spend the night on a rather comfortable divan in the adjoining sitting room, watching the view. Just thinking of spending the rest of his life next to a wife gave him the creeps. He had done his duty and if it were up to him, they wouldn't be spending much time together at all.

A good Indian wife could be expected to put up with her husband's whims. At least that's what he had witnessed all his life. His mother was no more happy being married to his father than he was being married to her. Yet, they had produced three sons in thirty-eight years and had somehow managed to cohabit peacefully all this time. If they could do it, there was no reason why he couldn't do the same.

Okay, Maribel would get somewhat of a raw deal, but a comfortable life was guaranteed. Most importantly, Deepak could do as he pleased and his father would be off his back.

Just that since the wedding and the discussion he'd had with Maribel in Chennai, Deepak felt edgier with every time he came close to his wife. How would he survive their honeymoon in South Africa? Two weeks of virtually never getting away from her! Thankfully, there were so many things to do and the clubs in Cape Town were legendary. With some luck, Maribel would be too tired to want sex anyway.

There was another problem, though. Robert Peele was no longer there to assist with his backup plan. Robert, who had owed him a huge debt, had fallen to his death from the veranda of his lavish mansion. Stupid man. Everything had been going so well. The hitman Robert had introduced him to, had also disappeared. Now it was up to Deepak Misra to make his own arrangements.

*

"Ladies, may I present the data contents of your water-damaged cell phone."

Jono held up a smartphone he had connected to one of his computers in the cottage. Lerato's phone lay disembowelled next to a melée of cables and plugs on the table. The two women clapped their hands.

"Oh, my bestest brother!" Charlie embraced Jono and gave him a smacking kiss on the forehead. "Could you save the images and recordings?"

"Thank you, thank you. And the pictures... I'm not even going to comment on the pictures Lerato took with a male friend..."

"Hey, we were at a public swimming pool with friends, if you must know."

"Be that as it may..." Jono continued, "I have recovered the data. Unfortunately, your phone could not be rescued. You have to be more careful. Don't drop it, but if you must, choose a carpet, not the floor or swimming pool or a bucket with dirty water."

"Yes, I'll try to keep that in mind, Mr. Computer Nerd, to whom I'm extremely grateful. Now I need to get myself a new phone."

"Yup. It was pure luck. Water and electronics don't go well together."

"What do I owe you?"

"Oh, a hug and dinner sometime?"

"You got it. You can have the hug right now. Dinner, later."

For the next two hours, they went through their evidence again.

"We've got him!" Lerato Gwala punched the air and looked up from her laptop screen. "Maribel Misra's aunt forwarded e-mails that prove he was involved in Mrs. Peele's killing. There are the photographs we took of the door to the hidden passage under the mansion, and now we can also prove that he was in touch with Robert Peele and a suspected hitman. We know that because we've retrieved the audio. Not bad for starters. I'll let Andy know how far we've come."

"Now we just need the name of the hitman."

"I'm sure he'll be able to trace the man's identity. In one of the e-mails, Misra refers to an even earlier hit."

Charlie knelt on the floor next to her with Popcorn on her lap. The little dog yelped when Lerato started shouting,

"It's alright, Poppie," Charlie said and patted the pooch. Billie tried to climb onto her lap next to Popcorn. The two dogs growled at each other, then decided to share the space. "Perfect. What did you find in the emails?"

"Listen to this: 'Hi Deepak, good to hear that

you've organised someone to do the dirty work again. You know what I mean. Even if it's a different guy this time. Shooting someone isn't pretty and I'm sure the new guy knows what he's doing if he comes recommended by your father. It must be quick and painless. Sarah will never feel a thing.' And that's just one badly disguised message. Deepak Misra answers these messages cryptically. 'Surgeons are unpredictable.' For instance."

"Did you say this surgeon comes recommended by Misra's father?"

"Mmhm." Lerato scrolled through the messages again. "Yes, that's how I understand it. Messed things up with the poor woman."

"Oh boy," Jono said. "I wonder how many people they have whacked. Anybody seen my screwdriver?"

"That's one way to put it," Charlie scolded him.

"The screwdriver is over there." Lerato pointed to the floor and kept scrolling. "I suppose you don't get this rich without some casualties along the way."

"Anybody want tea or coffee?" Jono asked and walked into the small open-plan kitchen to pour water into the kettle.

"I'd love some tea," Charlie said and gave Billie a good tummy-scratch.

"I'm still good, thanks though." Lerato kept scrolling. "In another message, our guy makes arrangements with Robert Peele to meet him and somebody called James Smith at the airport in P E. Obviously, a fake name. Gives a flight number, coming from Joburg and everything. Just two days before the murder of his wife."

"Conniving bastards. That's why the police couldn't find Deepak Misra's name on the passenger list. They used fake names." The kettle chirped.

Lerato nodded. "And then this: 'Hope things have gone according to plan-' and the answer is, 'Worth his weight in gold. You never know, I might need him again one day.' That's Robert Peele's answer, covering his arse and not naming the guy. So they used somebody from England coming with Misra. Maybe worth some more research, if old Mr. Misra is also involved."

"We don't exactly have proof. It could be code. And isn't that a job for the police? It's our job to prevent Maribel Sharma from getting offed by her conniving husband. I think it's also pretty clear that there is someone else in Cape Town."

Charlie took the cup of tea Jono handed her. "Can we use any of this as evidence in court, should it come to that?"

"That's up to the lawyers," Lerato answered.

"Wasn't the idea to stop the guy from committing murder?" Jono asked. "Now you want to take him to court?"

"We need to be prepared, just in case. Saving Maribel is our priority. Maybe we can find an eye-witness who's prepared to make a statement."

"You mean the people, who work at the Peele mansion? I doubt it." Charlie took a sip of her tea. "Ouch, it's still hot."

"Sorry, sis. Maybe they can order polygraph tests," Jono chimed in.

"You mean the court? I doubt that they will re-open a cold case just for us. We just don't know yet, how this Mr. Smith – which is probably not his real name – was paid. But I'm sure, we'll be able to trace payments from both perps and request phone records. Should it ever come to that…"

"Okay, you're the expert. Just tell me what you need me to do," Charlie said.

"We've already found out that there is a connection between the murder in PE and a planned murder, and quite a bit of other proof. With that, I can approach my former police colleagues in Cape Town and ask them to help."

"Will they listen to you?"

"I think so. I also need to give Maribel's aunt - my client – feedback soon. I hope she's impressed with us."

"Hmm, something about your client doesn't gel with me." Charlie creased her forehead.

"What do you mean? She's already paid in advance, so she's obviously serious about the case. And she's given us proof that Deepak Misra is a dirtbag."

"I can't put my finger on it, but something's not right."

"Now you tell me! That's not a whole lot to go on, Charlie."

"I know. Sorry. Maybe it's nothing."

"Alright then. I'll give her feedback and we'll take it from there."

"The plot begins to thicken," Jono said and sipped his coffee.

Chapter ELEVEN

The necktie was a swirl of silver and blue silk. He tried to do a simple knot in front of the large mirror in their beautiful honeymoon suite. Deepak Misra would not have bothered with it in this heat, but it was a gift from his mother and he needed to please her with a selfie.

He hated the heat and saw that stains were already forming under his armpits. Perhaps he should change his silk shirt first… he loosened the tie.

Somebody had given them a framed picture of them both in traditional clothing, smiling for the camera and insisted that Maribel put it in her suitcase. It was positioned next to the mirror, staring at him, reminding him that his decision to get married would haunt him for the rest of his life.

Happy pictures of their wedding day in Chennai stared back at him on their joint Instagram profile and now also happy pictures of their honeymoon in Cape Town. Deepak sighed with frustration. This wedding had turned into never-ending torture for him. Let's get this over with.

"Hurry up Maribel, the theatre is not going to wait for us." Deepak Misra pranced around in front of the mirror in a new shirt and tied the knot again. To him, the tie was a symbol of their young marriage: expensive and too tight. This business of getting married and acting like a caring husband was not up his alley - at all.

Maribel was pretty enough, kind and educated. A master's degree was something to be proud of if one cared for such things. It was something he could show off, should they return to Reading in two weeks time. Would they return together? He was honestly not sure of it yet.

It all depended on how things unfolded in Cape Town. It wasn't easy to set up his backup plan, in case it was needed. And then there was the little problem of producing at least one child to appease his parents. It all depended on how bearable Maribel would make it for him.

The plan would kick in only in case she proved too difficult to handle. These few weeks already seemed like an eternity. He looked at his watch. It was just after six and they were supposed to phone him at six to make first contact… Robert Peele had been his plan B. After all he'd done for him, Robert should have taken this one little thing off his hands. But no, he had fallen to his death off his veranda stone drunk. What a pillock!

Sometimes the pressure got to him. Last night Maribel had waited up. Apparently, the sight-seeing tour and a walk through the Company Gardens had not been tiring enough. She'd tried to take his shirt off! He'd clenched his teeth and pleaded exhaustion, the heat and that they had a long day ahead of them tomorrow, but Maribel hadn't been too happy about the rejection.

'I just want to be close to you," she'd sulked. "One might think that you don't like being close to me.'

'Just give it time…'

'When I said I'd wait, I didn't mean forever.'

He hadn't even lied about the exhaustion. Just that it wasn't from the heat in the Mother City. The reason went by the name of Gunther and he couldn't let her see him without taking a shower first. She thought that taking a walk to clear his head at the end of the day, was just something he did. She didn't ask questions, which proved that she could be trained. But was he right about that? Deepak worried that he wouldn't be able to hide his true feelings much longer and the more he managed to soften up his new wife, the better his prospects.

He glanced at the framed picture again while finally getting his tie done. Everybody had said that they were a beautiful couple during those seven endless days in England. Family and friends, his father's business partners and total strangers had celebrated their union at a local events venue. Deepak had enjoyed being the centre of attention and not much else.

All that money could have been put to better use. Apart from his trust fund, Deepak could always count on his father's wealth. Although he knew that Maribel didn't like slackers, he had managed to convince her he was in an important position at his father's export company.

True that he popped into the office now and again and sat in meetings or checked calculations when his father asked him to. But his father's attempt to groom his youngest son to be the businessman he wanted him to be, had failed so far. Deepak simply lacked ambition.

"Could you please close the zip on my dress, Deepak, love? Where are you?"

He hated it when she called him things like love and darling.

She walked into the room. "Ah, there you are, darling!" Maribel spun around in front of him posing in the new figure-hugging shift dress with a deep neckline. The sexy dress he'd helped pick out in that sinfully expensive boutique in Sea Point. Maribel turned to face him. "And?"

"And what?" He asked.

"How do I look? Do you still like it as much on me as you did in the store?"

"I like it even better now," Deepak said and forced a smile without missing a beat.

She was so pretty. So very pretty and so very undesirable.

They had known absolutely nothing about each other when they met and he knew that it was meant to be that way. Put a pot with cold water on the stove and it will boil throughout the marriage. How often had he been subjected to this wisdom of the older generation?

Just that nothing about Maribel could have made his blood as hot and glowing as the mere sight of Gunther or Alec did. Gunther was not his only skilled lover at the brothel in Long Street he frequented, but the most satisfying one.

Cape Town was turning out more exciting than he could have hoped for. Maribel didn't know how lucky she was that he had this pressure release valve. The thought of Gunther literally took his breath away. Maybe he could organise a visit after the theatre and dinner tonight…

Now he had to go to plan C and organise things by himself. He'd lost track of the two women in Port Elizabeth after they'd left the guesthouse in Humewood quite suddenly. The strange thing was… he thought he'd recognised them near the hotel yesterday and although he couldn't say for sure that they were in town because of him, he couldn't risk those bitches foiling his plan C.

Damn bad luck that David had been shot dead

before he could take care of this one last job for him. Thank goodness they'd shot him dead and didn't just wound him, he thought to himself, dead men can't talk! And neither can dead women.

So he'd set his new contact, Thutso, on them. Thutso drove the hotel minibus and used his private motorbike to follow them in his spare time. Deepak was paying well and the driver had been more than happy to comply.

Whoever had hired these women, would not find out about his almost nightly visits to The Den if he could help it. The phone call had been about getting rid of them and, if unavoidable, getting rid of his wife. He was not sure that he wanted to remove Maribel permanently from his life.

She was useful in many ways, but last night she'd lost her cool. Why couldn't she just let him be and play the obedient wife he had hoped for? Hopefully, there wouldn't be a repeat of their ugly spat. Today, all had been forgiven and forgotten, but it was early days.

"I'll just finish my make-up, then I'm ready to go." Maribel seemed excited about going to the theatre. A famous musical show for which he had booked front row tickets months ago was in town.

His cell phone beeped and Deepak Misra felt as excited as if Gunther himself had just walked right through the door. It was them!

"Let me get that. Don't take too long with your makeup, Maribel."

"I'll be done in two ticks."

She chuckled and got to work in the bathroom of the holiday suite. Deepak swiftly walked through the sitting room and out onto the balcony. The traffic noise would obscure his conversation. 'Yes, I can talk,' he said and lowered his voice. Deepak pressed the phone to his ear. 'What have you got for me?' Let's get it over and done with, he thought.

'Sure, no problem. But that's too soon. I still have to go to the bank and… Yes of course I'll do that. Yes, I should have the money by then. That's more than we discussed…'

He calculated the amount back to Pound Stirling and it was really peanuts to him. 'Very well, but you will wait until I give you the sign. Good. As long as we are clear about that. No, you don't need to know that. And it is only a deposit at this stage. The rest on completion. Can we meet in the hotel lobby?'

"What are you doing outside, darling? It's so very noisy." Maribel suddenly stood in the sliding door. He hadn't closed it but felt like doing it right now, squashing her like a bothersome bug. The violent thought subsided. She must be the only woman on the planet, who did her makeup this quickly.

'Okay, got to go.' He hung up. How long had she been standing there? Had Maribel heard any part of his conversation with the go-between?

He smiled affably. "Nearly done. Are you ready to beetle?" The look on her face answered his silent questions.

"What are you doing, Deepak? Why do you have to pay somebody cash in the hotel lobby?"

At that moment, he knew that he would never be free if he stayed married to this woman. He would always have to look over his shoulder, would always have to explain himself. Alec had been right all along. Ball and chain… ball and chain…

"Ah, it's nothing Maribel, just paying for the trip out to the coast tomorrow morning. He charges me a special price and wants it in cash."

"Alright, I see." She wasn't so sure about it. Why was he trying to hide the conversation from her? But she didn't want to spoil things tonight.

"Ready when you are, love."

"I'm ready as I'll ever be."

*

Charlie and Lerato sat in a hired car and observed the entrance to the hotel. A real nice place Deepak Misra and his bride had chosen for their honeymoon. They had been on their stakeout after the couple had left at about twenty past six.

Now, the Misras had returned. Beautiful Maribel had looked rather tired, but Deepak re-appeared after thirty minutes and got onto the back of a motorbike. Lerato guessed that the driver was Thutso, a hotel employee. He would probably take Deepak Misra to the brothel in Long Street again.

"There he is, Charlie. Okay, let's follow him." Lerato turned the key and the engine roared. "I'll never get the hang of these hired cars."

Charlie had been watching people walking past. "What? Where?"

"See that guy in sunglasses and helmet on the back

of that motorbike?" Lerato tried to stay as close to the bike as she dared without being detected.

"Yes, but I can't see his face."

"You don't have to. He's wearing the same suit he did when they arrived back at the hotel."

Charlie stretched her neck. "You're right, but who needs sunglasses at this hour?" She sniggered. "It's already dark."

The motorbike took a right-hand turn and the sleuths followed. There wasn't much traffic in the quiet back streets and Lerato hung back, letting in a family car. "Maybe he thinks it's a great disguise. Who knows?"

"Thank goodness you know what you're doing. I wouldn't have seen him."

"I'll say." Lerato turned at a traffic light and drove up the hill.

"Do you think he knows that he's being followed?"

"I hope not, but he is no stranger to crime. He might have a sixth sense for things like that." They had found out that the old Mr. Misra did not always run his business by the book, and an apple doesn't fall far from the tree…

"Let's hope he is a criminal without a sixth sense. That's my department." Charlie said this in a flippant sort of way, but both of them knew that there was a grain of truth in it.

They followed the bike down the hill and into the centre of town. If Deepak wanted to visit the brothel, this was a rather strange route. The bike turned off sooner than expected and was halfway up the hill again. Lerato followed at a safe distance when a red car pushed in between them. That wasn't necessarily a bad thing, as long as they didn't lose sight of the bike. The red car drove on, just as the bike with their suspect stopped at a very small shopping centre.

Lerato drove past the shops and parked behind another car. They could still see the bike and their suspect from here.

"What do they want at a corner shop, a vacuum cleaner place and a Chinese Take-Away? Conduct some shady deal?" Charlie wondered.

"Wish I knew." Lerato switched the headlights off. The road was dark except for the lights at the shopping centre. "Maybe he's still hungry after his fancy dinner."

"Then why are they not getting off the bike?"

"Good question."

"Maybe they did notice us?"

"Could be, but I was careful." She inserted the car key in the ignition just in case. They saw two men come out of the Chinese Take-Away and walk towards the bike.

"Did you see them greet the driver?" Charlie asked. "I'm smelling a rat."

"They don't even have takeaway food with them, so why did they come out of the Chinese place? Let's get moving. They are coming towards us." Lerato tried to start the sputtering motor. "Damn, what now? Don't let me down, car!"

The two men approached and the car still struggled to start. "Come on!"

As if the car had heard Lerato's plea, it started just in time! The men were running now as they turned back into the road with screeching tyres, narrowly missing one of the men, who kept running next to the car. Someone fired a shot. Glass shattered and an alarm went off, but it wasn't them. The shot must have hit another car.

"They are after us, Lerato!" Charlie shrieked and ducked instinctively.

"That's what you call a hitman? Lousy routine," Lerato hissed contemptuously and kept her eyes on the road.

"Thank God for that!" Charlie cried. She stole a glance in the rear mirror. "There are people in the street now. They won't risk shooting at us again, will they?"

Lerato tried to get away from the scene and turned into a road going down the hill.

"How must I know? Hang on, I'll try to get some space between us and those lousy shots," Lerato warned her friend. They zigzagged through the steep streets she knew from her time in Cape Town until they could be fairly certain that nobody was following them. Lerato slowed down and parked their hired car close to the main road that led directly into town. She checked the mirrors then took her gun out of the holster and released the safety catch.

"Don't tell me you want to start shooting at them!"

"Only if absolutely necessary." Lerato sounded scarily calm.

A black limousine zoomed past and waited at the

red traffic light.

"F**k what if it was them? Maybe they changed their vehicle…" Charlie whispered just as a couple came out of a doorway. The sudden movement startled Lerato and held her gun still at the ready. The couple walked past arm in arm, laughing.

"We'll wait for a while, just to make sure." she said and relaxed. The traffic light changed to amber, then green and the limousine drove on.

"Good! It seems we've lost them," she said after some tense waiting. "Bloody hell, that devious bastard! It was a trap! A f**king trap. And I fell for it."

"How were you supposed to know that he wanted to lure us to that shopping centre? Plus, he does seem to have a sixth sense."

"I should not have been so complacent. He's already hired hitmen! I'll have to give Dora Kwame a call. She's got plenty of experience with situations like this."

"Who's Dora Kwame?"

"She's a police investigator. Former colleague. They fired at us. That's a crime, as far as I remember."

Charlie breathed deeply to calm her nerves. "He was testing these guys on us," she said. "He's on his way to the brothel now. Wouldn't have cared either way if we got shot back there, but I think he wanted to give us a warning to stay away."

"Damn, I can't get hold of Dora." Lerato stared at her cell phone and tried again.

"She's probably driving."

"How do you know that? Oh, why am I even asking? You could have given me a heads up when we were following the bike. Was there no smoke or mist hanging around?"

"Lerato, I'm not psychic. That was different... I'm just taking a wild guess here."

"Never mind. If he's getting hitmen involved, that means he might be planning something else with those goons." Lerato dialled Dora Kwame's number again. "Engaged!" She sounded frustrated.

"Now all we have to do is find out how and when the hijacking is going down," Charlie said and tried to remember details from her dream. "Well, we know that he's using the van to travel to Cape Point tomorrow."

"But how do we find out when they are going? I'm not keen to get taken out by those gangsters for snooping around."

"I don't know what day it was in my dream, but it must have been late morning, judging by the position of the sun. Not quite noon yet."

"That's pretty detailed. I'm impressed, lady, and it doesn't give us much time!" Lerato dialled again.

'Dora? Hi, yes it's me, Lerato. Sorry to call you so late. You're driving?" She gave Charlie a stern look. "I'm fine, apart from the fact that we were just shot at somewhere between Greenpoint and Signal Hill. No, we drove away, but another car was hit. Yes. Yes. That must be it. A small shopping centre on the hill. Chinese Take-Away and a store with vacuum cleaners. You know which one? Good. No, we are somewhere in Fresnaye now. They didn't follow us or we lost them. Can you send a team out? That's even better…'

"Tell her that he's planning something soon."

'We believe that the suspect we were following is up to something… to get rid of his wife. Remember, I told you about the case? Yes, I know it was up in the air back then. Yes, it's unusual, that's why we're in town. We think it's going down tomorrow. Same perps. Thanks, you're the best! Hang on....' Lerato gave Dora the address of The Den, where Deepak Misra very likely was.

"What did she say?" Charlie demanded to know.

"They will tail him and send a team to the Chinese Take-Away place where they shot at us. She said we must go back there and give a statement, then come to the station tomorrow morning at about 8 o'clock. She'll be back on duty and organise something. Thank god the woman has vision!"

"That's good news! Can we get out of here, please?"

"Sure, but I want to hear everything you remember from your dream. We need to give Dora Kwame something to work with." Lerato Gwala started the car and reversed into the next driveway. "This is getting serious."

*

Maribel Misra awoke from her slumber as their van pulled into a secluded parking bay by the mountain to take a break. They were on their way to Cape Point and would spend the day on the far southern tip of the continent. Her cheeks were flushed and she moaned a little. Maribel had dreamed about happily dancing with her new husband in a Bollywood movie: mere dilé haré haré…

He had picked up his bride and swirled her around only to set her down and look deep into her eyes, full of desire. Maribel sighed and sat up.

There was a viewing platform across the road. Perhaps they could go there while they waited. The last few days of their honeymoon had been filled with fabulous activities and the tired young bride took naps whenever she could.

She didn't know it yet, but her new husband had no intention of taking in the magnificent view or of going to Cape Point for the day. Not after last night's argument! This time, she had caught him speaking to his lover and tormented him with questions.

Enough was enough! He felt sorry for her, but not sorry enough to let her live.

Right now, Deepak was concerned that there could be other cars around when things went down. The last thing he needed was witnesses. He had decided to give the guys another chance after last night's dismal performance. He didn't have much of a choice as Maribel was getting too troublesome.

Deepak scanned the road all the way to the horizon. No cars. He could see a red-striped sleeve peeking out from behind one of the rocks. Good, he thought with relief. Plan C was set in motion.

*

"Can't you put your foot down?" Lerato Gwala urged the driver of the undercover police vehicle. They were zooming up the mountain road towards Cape Point and were still far from the spot Charlie had seen in her dream.

"Madam, I'm doing what I can," the young policeman answered. Lerato leaned back with a deep sigh as he stuck to the speed limit.

The Misras were clueless that the police were making every effort to catch up with the minivan Deepak had hired for the day. They had left the hotel just before 9:30 am and Mr. Misra seemed in a rather cheerful mood.

He'd finalised the deal only this morning. The argument his wife had started last night had been the straw that broke the camel's back. It had all come out because she couldn't stay out of his business.

The police were notified about the argument. They also knew about the plan to take the hotel's van out to the coast, so Dora Kwame had jumped into action.

Another undercover vehicle was closely following the van along the winding road to Cape Point and they had joined the pursuit about 40 minutes later.

If there were more suspects involved, they would need backup right away. So, Detective Sergeant Dora Kwame was constantly in contact with the police officers in the other vehicle. 'Anything yet?' She spoke firmly into her cell phone.

'Making visual contact. Still going below the speed limit,' came the prompt answer.

"Okay, we're catching up with you."

There were only two places that had qualified as a possible target and a tracking device they had affixed to the hotel van confirmed that the place they were heading for was the second of two viewing platforms along the road.

'We can see you now.'

'Okay, keep us updated. We are passing through the first location.'

'Roger.'

Dora Kwame had worked with Lerato Gwala long enough to know that she'd never waste her time for no good reason. According to their observations of the suspect's actions last night and this morning, they had reason to intervene. At the station, they had gone over the map again, based on details an 'unidentified informer' had provided. Now at least, they had a projected crime scene.

The informant was, of course, Charlie Proudfoot. They had described the viewing platform and rock wall at the location.

An undercover police officer, posing as a deliveryman, had found out that the newlyweds were indeed on their way to Cape Point for a day trip and that they wouldn't be back until late evening. The police jumped into gear with uncommon swiftness. The fact that foreigners had been using the Mother City as a backdrop to similar crimes for some time, was spurring them on.

"Dora, please tell him to go faster." Lerato felt nervous now. She and Charlie were riding in the vehicle with the seasoned policewoman.

"Don't get worked up. At best, we'll stop the perps from committing murder. At worst, we'll catch them in the act." Dora Kwame put her hand on Lerato's arm.

"That guy is just so unpredictable. Remember what they tried to do to us last night?"

Charlie kept quiet. At some level, she knew that the murder hadn't happened yet, but she couldn't forget the nightmare she'd lived through so many times before. They approached the first rest stop. Two cars were parked close to the road and people were admiring the view.

"It's the next stop," Dora Kwame said and pointed down the road. "Not too much traffic today, we should be there soon."

"That's another 10 kilometers to go," Lerato groaned. "It's going to take too long."

"Should I drive faster, Madam?" The constable asked his superior officer.

Dora Kwame nodded. "Step on it, Ronald."

*

"I have to go to the toilet quickly."

Maribel Misra thought that the driver's voice sounded a bit strange, but she might be mistaken. Why should the driver of the hotel's mini-van sound strange?

"Darling, I dreamed that…" she began to address her husband. He sat next to her and smiled with such a strange expression. "What's going on?"

A driver, who sounded strange and a husband, who smiled at her in an odd way… wasn't that too much of a coincidence? Maribel moved away from Deepak and held her handbag in front of her chest as if to protect herself.

"What do you mean?" Her husband stopped smiling.

"Something is up, I can feel it."

"You're imagining things, dear," Deepak Misra assured her. He never used terms of endearment. Wasn't it a reason to be glad?

"Am I really?" She was suddenly not so sure anymore. Deepak had no reason to lie to her. Then she heard voices outside the van. "Who is the driver speaking to?"

A red car drove past them, followed by a motorbike. Deepak followed them with his eyes. Good, they were minding their own business.

"I don't know, maybe someone he knows?" He said.

"In the middle of nowhere? And what's that noise

all about?"

"What noise?" Deepak was so focused on his goal that he blended out the noise she was referring to.

"I hear nothing." He got up and checked why the men were not making the move they had discussed.

Maribel sat rigidly upright and doubt crept back into her mind. "Don't you hear the sirens?" The blaring noise intensified.

"What sirens?" Where are the guys? He thought angrily, what's keeping them? But then he couldn't ignore the sound of police sirens any longer. Two more cars passed the viewing platform in short succession.

"Shit, shit, shit." His face took on a hunted expression. "Hurry up, you morons!" He shouted. Suddenly the driver stood behind him.

"We cannot do that, sir. The police are coming," Thutso refused.

"Then give me the iron! I'll do it myself," Deepak Misra hissed at him. He wanted to get the job done. This is what they had come for. To rid him of his biggest problem. Now they wouldn't get their second payment. Cheapest hit ever. The consequences of his actions didn't even cross his mind.

The sound of screeching tyres jolted Deepak from his void. Another two cars hurtled towards them, but they didn't pass. There was nothing remarkable about the first one. The second car was undeniably a police van.

"Sir, you cannot… sir!" The driver cried.

A frightened Thutso Ndima stuck the pistol into the back of his pants… and that's where the police found it when they searched the men on the scene. They made them stand with their arms outstretched against the side of the police van, legs apart. They also found a motorbike parked against the overhang and questioned the men.

Deepak Misra was angry that his plan had failed. It had been a good plan. He had done his best, but everybody else had let him down! Deepak let himself fall onto the front seat and when the police entered the vehicle, he feigned shock and outrage.

"Thank you for saving us," he cried. "Another minute and it would have been too late. It was the driver. Him!" He pointed to Thutso Ndima. "These, these other men were hiding behind the rocks. They wanted to rob us!"

"Is that so?" Dora Kwame asked calmly. "Is that true, Mrs. Misra?"

Deepak looked confused. "You know who we are?"

"You came just in time…" The young woman began to sob.

"It's alright." Dora Kwame said. "We know that madam."

The police officers outside put handcuffs on the amateurish contract killers. The three men did not resist when they were ordered to sit on the ground.

"Please call me Ms Sharma," Maribel cried. "I've never really been married to this man. This monster! It was all a sham. He wanted to kill me!"

"Calm yourself, Maribel. You don't know what you're saying," Deepak said unsteadily. "What are you doing? It's all a big misunderstanding."

His wife glared at him. "A misunderstanding? How can '…give me the iron, I'll do it myself...' be a misunderstanding?" She started crying and searched for a tissue in her handbag.

"Sorry about my wife," Deepak Misra carried on in the same vein as before. "It really is a misunderstanding. She is in shock. Get that off me!"

"I apologise," Dora Kwame said. "The handcuffs are procedure. Premeditated murder is a serious crime and we must secure all possible suspects."

"Premeditated murder? What are you talking about?"

"The fact that you conspired to murder your wife," Lerato Gwala said and smiled.

"I knew something was strange when I woke up just now!"

"Maribel, you can't be serious. I would never hurt you, you know that."

"Oh but you would, Deepak, you would!" The pretty young woman leaned over and gave her husband a sound slap. "You must be some kind of psycho to do this. Just because I found out about your lover in England? Do you really think I would have stayed married to you after what you just did? You would have killed me! 'Hurry up you morons. Give me the iron, I'll do it myself.' That's what you said."

She dried her tears that didn't want to stop flowing, smudging her makeup.

"You must have dreamed it, darling. Remember, you were asleep when the van stopped..." Deepak Misra flashed a bright smile at the detective sergeant, despite his smarting cheek.

His wife would have none of it. "Some nightmare, getting married to you," she sobbed. Rubbing her eyes with the tissue made her makeup run even worse. Lerato took a tissue and helped her clean up the streaks.

"What?! She is lying to you, officer. I would never… my wife… she…" Deepak Misra was searching for words.

"Take him out of here," the detective said with undeniable contempt. One of the officers led him away. "Please come this way, Mr. Misra."

"I will lodge a complaint." The young man became furious again. "You will regret this! Treating innocent visitors to your country in this way. I swear my father will leave no stone unturned to get me off the hook."

"Careful with that head of yours," the policeman said and pushed Mr. Misra's head gently below the doorframe.

"Don't you dare touch me! Did you see how he touched me?"

"Just shut up you pathetic arse." The young bride didn't mince her words. "I can't believe I was so stupid as to accept your proposal and go through with that... sham of a wedding. Impotent, my foot! I should have known better. When you dance with the devil..." she took a deep breath, but Deepak was already out of earshot.

"How could you know what was going to happen?" Maribel suddenly addressed Dora Kwame.

Her light-blue linen dress was damp and creased, but there were none of the sticky, red stains. Charlie noticed this with a feeling of satisfaction. The nightmare had not played out in reality.

"Solid policework, Mrs. Misra, sorry... I mean Sharma," the police detective said. "Our police force may be overworked and underpaid, but sometimes we do get it right. And you can thank an informant, who contacted these two PIs."

"An informant?" Maribel asked confused.

"That's for another day," Lerato answered.

Hopefully, that day would never come.

Chapter TWELVE

As soon as the news hit the headlines, the press made a dive for the story. The son of a British millionaire was accused of planning to kill his new bride and blame it on South Africa's crime statistics?

This story stirred up even more public interest than the American cokehead who'd callously murdered his girlfriend at a luxury hotel just two months before.

The focus shifted swiftly from the crime statistics in South Africa to the two-timing husband. Deepak Misra vehemently denied any involvement in the attempted murder, before his attorney advised him not to speak to anyone. His father, Ashwin Misra, at once hired one of the top attorneys in Cape Town through a contact, and this attorney knew all the tricks in the book.

The statements of his three alleged accomplices contradicted his version in almost everything. They pointed to him as the mastermind of the plot that never came to fruition. Lie detector tests were ordered.

The tests were administered by a polygraph expert

from Johannesburg, but Deepak Misra's results proved inconclusive. Rumour had it that his attorney knew how to outsmart the procedure. But proving that was quite another matter.

Footage gleaned from CCTV cameras in the hotel lobby, showed how Deepak Misra had handed an envelope with money to the driver and spoke to two of the co-accused. The video clip went viral on social media and TV stations played it over and over on the news.

Of course, he claimed that it had just been a payment for the trip to Cape Point and that nothing sinister had been discussed. He only knew the driver. Back in the hotel lobby, the other man had been introduced to him as his cousin. These men had planned the robbery all by themselves. Why the police accused him of conspiring to his wife's murder was beyond him.

The attorney worked his expensive magic and the main suspect was released on bail, which had been set at 500,000 Rand. This was a small fortune in South Africa, but not in England, where a PR whizz was hired as the Misra family's spokesperson.

Deepak Misra was allowed to leave for his native Great Britain and ordered to return for the trial.

Somehow, the spokesman managed to make Deepak appear as an innocent victim caught up in a miscarriage of justice in a Third World country that was known for its brutal police force and unbearable prisons. The story would hold the attention of the public for many months to come.

As soon as the accused set foot on British soil, he was whisked away in a black limousine, leaving reporters and camera teams at the mercy of the snarky PR man, who answered their questions as evasively as possible. Deepak had allegedly committed himself to a psychiatric clinic close to his hometown as he was afflicted by some mysterious mental illness. Reporters questioned this and whether he was not simply hiding from justice.

What followed was a rehearsed speech in front of TV cameras, claiming that the young man was overwhelmed by the mistrust his new wife had extended to him. He was also being treated for the after-effects of post-traumatic stress caused by the attempted robbery and by the treatment he'd been subjected to in South Africa.

The newspapers were full of speculations and the

news ran live reports about the attempted murder case that was unfolding in Cape Town.

Maribel Misra's family hired an attorney, whose résumé was just as impressive as her husband's lawyer's. After she'd told police all she could about the case, Maribel flew back to Switzerland and remained in Zurich until the trial.

The couple had seemed so happy about the lavish wedding and the merging of the two families. Now there was no love lost between the Sharmas and the Misras. Especially since Deepak's father open declaration that he might sue Maribel's father for half the wedding expenses in Chennai, as he now didn't have a daughter-in-law to show for the money he'd spent.

Over his dead body would his youngest son be extradited to face investigations in South Africa with such horrific dangers lurking around every corner!

Nobody seemed concerned that the three co-accused remained in custody and weren't afforded the same leniency as the British citizen.

In Cape Town, justice took its course and the three suspects appeared before the High Court. During the trial, they unanimously pointed to Deepak Misra as the instigator of the unsuccessful murder plot and no, there had been no robbery.

It was decided to separate the court proceedings and the three co-accused appeared first. The public followed the trial on a daily basis.

"Mr. Ndima, didn't you also arrange for hitmen to wait at a Chinese Take-Away in Thornhill Road for the private detectives who were following you? There was a shot fired, as far as I remember," the prosecutor asked the driver.

"Sir?"

"Would you like me to repeat the question, Mr. Ndima?" The taxi driver nodded, obviously rattled, and the prosecutor repeated his question to the Xhosa interpreter.

"I… emm… yes, I was driving Mr. Misra to a Chinese Take-Away in Greenpoint on my motorbike and somebody shot at a car, but I don't know who that was. I drove away quickly because we were afraid."

"Really? And you want us to believe that you had nothing to do with the incident?"

"Yes, sir." The interpreter translated.

"So these private investigators who followed Mr.

Misra on a tip-off, are shot at in a place where you just happen to stop by chance and then you drive off without notifying the police of the shooting?"

"Yes."

"Can you at least give the court a description of the gunmen and what you saw?"

"No sir, I was scared and Mr. Misra said to drive away." Thutso Ndima didn't look at the prosecutor once and kept touching his mouth while answering the questions. But he wasn't let off the hook so easily.

"I see. So, you didn't know that the gunmen were waiting at the location that Mr. Misra told you to take him? It was all a coincidence?"

Thutso Ndima didn't seem too sure about his answer. Moments went by.

"Yes."

"That doesn't make much sense, Mr. Ndima. Are you saying that it was pure coincidence that you happened to drive Mr. Misra to the location of the shooting?"

"Yes." The driver wrung his hands, sweating visibly.

"If that is your statement, it will be recorded as such." The prosecutor addressed the presiding judge.

"My Lord, ballistic evidence proves that the gun Mr. Ndima had on his person when he was arrested, was a perfect match to the bullet and casing we found in a blue Volkswagen Beetle on the scene of the shooting. The gunmen narrowly missed the car of private investigators Lerato Gwala and Charlie Proudfoot. I think we can safely assume that there is a connection between the two incidents."

The driver looked at his shoes while the prosecutor made this statement. Afterwards, his co-accused stated that they had received a deposit of 2,000 Rand each for the hit at the Chinese Take-Away and had never been paid in full.

"He wanted us to make up for not killing the women, and Thutso made a new deal with him." The interpreter translated, while the driver hung his head in shame.

Charlie and Lerato were never called as witnesses and the three accused were sentenced to lengthy jail terms.

Since they had implicated Deepak Misra, all eyes were now on him. Was he, or wasn't he, guilty of masterminding the murder plot? The public couldn't wait for the truth to come out.

Then it became known that the British man

accused was not planning to return to South Africa in order to stand trial. The public was furious. The rich always get away with murder, was the consensus of most who followed the trial.

An extradition order was applied for by the South African government. This could take months and caused even more drama. It didn't help that the Minister of the Police called the accused 'one of those monkeys who come to South Africa to commit crimes'.

To add to Deepak Misra's troubles, the case in Port Elizabeth was reopened.

A new detective by the name of Abraham van Uys took over and Dora Kwame arranged for the evidence Lerato and Charlie unearthed to be forwarded to him.

The detective in Port Elizabeth could immediately identify the man at the clandestine meeting with Robert Peele and Deepak Misra at the seafood restaurant from the photographs. He was a well-known criminal.

"We can confirm that the investigation in the case of Mrs. Sarah Peele's murder has been re-opened," Detective van Uys answered when asked about the status of the investigations. "I cannot divulge any details at this stage or how Mr. Misra was involved, but the investigation is progressing."

Lerato learned that Mr. Peele's former butler was being questioned by the police.

Mr. Lupo was currently employed by a local pastor and politician who had come into a great deal of money. The pastor experienced his very own run-in with the law. He was accused of money laundering, corruption, human trafficking, rape and kidnapping. Mr. Lupo saw his chance of getting out of trouble and sang like a canary.

His memory miraculously returned when he saw the pictures of the door to the secret passage below the mansion. He assured the detective that Mrs. Peele's killer must have left through that very passage as nobody could remember seeing him enter or leave the house. And what was more, the hitman's name was David Cruikshank.

He'd arrived from London together with Mr. Misra and they'd shared cocktails with Mr. Peele the night before the jewellery theft. Mr. Lupo also recognised the man in the restaurant photographs, because he himself had arranged for him to meet with his boss. Mr. Peele had asked him to find somebody who could carry out 'errands' and Mr. Lupo was well aware of what this meant. Very odd that Mr. Peele should fall to his death on the same day.

However, the butler never admitted to chasing the two women who had driven away from the mansion. When the police had a closer look at his mother's house, they found the brown Nissan parked behind a hedge, covered in old blankets. Since he had made a deal with the State, the charges, in this case, were dropped.

"Dramatic twist in the attempted murder saga involving British businessman Deepak Misra!!" The headlines screamed The public lapped up every morsel of it.

Lennart van Rooyen's name came up briefly. The retired detective had come out of his coma, but he was still in hospital and could not remember details of the previous investigation, or his assailants.

The Maitirelo PI agency was not mentioned in any of the news reports, but Lerato and Charlie were expected to be called as witnesses during Deepak Misra's trial, in case the extradition was granted. They had done their job and prevented a killer from getting away. Not bad for an unusual investigation like this one.

Their informant, however, had disappeared and there was also the small issue of the client, who had hired the PIs in the first place.

She was neither replying to phone calls nor messages and Interpol was unable to find her whereabouts.

"I wonder what's going on there," Lerato said to Charlie. "It would be best if she came to Cape Town for the trial against Misra, being Maribel Misra's aunt and all. Maybe she's already given a statement, but I'm sure that if she gave evidence in court, it would strengthen the case of the prosecution."

"You think that something happened to her?"

"Sho! I hope not."

Then Maribel's family announced in the news that she would be travelling to Cape Town with her mother and Aunt Aadiya Sharma. After months of speculation regarding Deepak Misra's mental state, he re-appeared looking sallow and confused. Would the extradition be granted, and was he able to stand trial in South Africa?

The Misra-family spokesman remained tight-lipped and the public was glued to their TV-screens.

A video of Deepak Misra bouncing his 3-year-old nephew on his knee appeared on Twitter. In the post, he was described as an innocent man, who loved nothing more than to spend time with his family.

Another video showed him serenading his mother-in-law at the wedding in Chennai.

The PR machine, hired to tip the scale in Deepak's favour, was in full motion.

Memes appeared online in response to the videos and other tweets. Instead of achieving public empathy, they'd turned Deepak into a laughing stock. The PR effort had failed to make the desired impact as the extradition of the young man was still up in the air.

While all of this grabbed public attention, an unlikely murder victim was discovered in the River Kennet in Berkshire, and this murder received barely any attention at the time.

The body of an undoubtedly Indian woman was found floating at the confluence with the River Thames, caught in branches by the shore. The coroner determined that she had been in the water for two weeks and that some form of torture had taken place shortly before her death.

It was established that the body had been weighed down with rocks tied around her abdomen, causing it to stay below the water surface. Who was this woman, where and why had the murder been committed? The answer to these questions was so unexpected that it would change the course of the Misra case.

The police in Berkshire established that the woman who had drowned in the Kennet River was one Prafula Dubey. She was a wealthy housewife in her fifties from Reading who was known for her devout demeanour.

Everyone who knew her was puzzled. The woman had clearly been murdered. What motive could possibly be behind the killing of a middle-aged Indian woman of good standing? Then it came to light that Mrs. Dubey had not been reported as missing for two weeks due to a misunderstanding.

Mr. Dubey had left on a business trip to India the same day and staff had assumed that he had done so in the company of his wife.

They didn't usually share their plans with the rest of the family, so her disappearance came to light only after Mr. Dubey's return to Reading. Her picture was matched to the naked, decomposing body that had been found in the small river. The husband was ruled out as a suspect, and the police were stumped.

Not long after the newspapers reported on the Berkshire case, a cleaning woman, who worked at a rather sordid establishment in London, came forward and stated that she'd recognised the woman on the telly.

She knew for a fact that Mrs. Dubey had serviced customers in a room at the establishment that she rented on a monthly basis - under the name Miss Whiplash.

She was a dominatrix for sure, the cleaner said, and yes she recognised one of her customers because he had also been on the telly often of late. The man she'd recognised was Deepak Misra!

At first, the police didn't take the cleaner's statement seriously and the Misra family did not even comment. Mr. Dubey was outraged at the suggestion of his wife's alleged double-life. That's when the case began to evoke interest.

The police decided to follow up on several leads, even the absurd notion that Mrs. Dubey could have rented a room at a downtown brothel.

After a thorough search of the room the cleaner indicated, they found a red notebook in Mrs. Dubey's handwriting under a creaky floorboard behind the metal-frame bed.

The many mirrors on the walls and the ceiling reflected the policemen's images as they studied the contents. S&M paraphernalia were later found in a gym bag in the victim's abandoned car. The notebook contained names and phone numbers of several well-to-do men, including Deepak Misra. This was treated as proof of a possible connection.

The cleaning woman asked for a reward and was informed that there was no reward. "So, why did I even tell you coppers?" She asked. "Cost me nothing but trouble, the whole affair."

She was referring to a number of death threats she had received. The woman went into hiding and the news hit the tabloids like a bomb.

Speculations began to churn. First in the local press, then nationwide.

Deepak Misra could not have committed the murder of Prafula Dubey, as he was in an institution at the time, but he had made use of the woman's sexual services. Suddenly the Misra case had a whole new spicy dimension to it.

The Indian community distanced itself from the Dubey-family without much ado. Many knew that the husband of the Berkshire murder-victim was involved in trade deals that sometimes were less than legal, so the motive was possibly retaliation.

The investigations went this way and that and eventually fizzled out.

The media lost interest in the case and the spotlight was firmly back on Deepak Misra and the extradition hearings. And they didn't have to wait long.

The extradition to South Africa was finally granted under strict conditions. Deepak Misra rendered himself numb with prescription drugs and arrived at Cape Town airport with a large entourage. He was greeted by a tsunami of reporters and flashlights. Once again, he found himself in this beautiful coastal city at the southern tip of Africa and was whisked away to a private location.

Everyone was convinced that justice would finally take its course.

"You see, I knew he wouldn't get away with it," Mr. Sharma said as his extended family In Zurich sat around the dinner table, discussing the news while eating Biryani. "You must just be brave now, Maribel. Everything will turn out alright."

"I will do my best, Papa. I just wish the whole thing was over already."

"Soon enough, and we will watch him go down in court," Aadiya Sharma said. Her niece had gone through enough turmoil following her ordeal in South Africa and the annulment of her marriage. Maribel managed a weak smile.

"I cannot see that the court won't convict this scoundrel after what he has done," her mother said. "You will truthfully tell the court what you know, as will the two private detectives and the policewoman, who rescued you."

Maribel turned to her father. "Oh Papa, I wish you could come with us."

"Ma chère, I'm sure your mother and aunt will look after you just fine. I have important business to attend to."

Alec, Deepak's lover in Crissenden Park, kept his

distance for fear of being dragged into the wretched case and this contributed to Deepak Misra's low mood. The young man was visibly squirming under public scrutiny.

When word of Prafula Dubey's murder reached him, Deepak's grief made itself known through volatile mood swings. With Alec, he had sated his lust, while his visits to Prafula had been the highlight of his weekly exploits in London.

She had been the forbidden fruit and only she knew how to satisfy his hankering for pain to the point where it gave way to an explosion of pleasure. Although he would never have called it love, these encounters made him feel alive. Now he would never see her again.

Dominatrix, bi-sexual, jealous – those were words that would give every other good and pious Indian housewife hives. And that's exactly how Deepak Misra's mother felt. She had met Prafula Dubey for lunch or the occasional garden party, and she'd always struck her as very prim and proper. On one such occasion, this woman must have approached her poor, innocent son.

In fact, those two had pretended to barely know each other! Her disappearance had been disconcerting, but who could have guessed at the truth? Deepak had been having a shameful affair with her right under his mother's nose. Outrageous!

*

In Cape Town, a large crowd was assembling in front of the High Court building. Many held up banners in support of the bride and against gender-based violence.

Cameras flashed away as Maribel Misra ascended the stairs. She gave a brief interview in front of one of the Greek columns.

"All I want is for the truth to come out. My soon-to-be ex-husband has returned from the UK to face justice. We have decided to go our separate ways. Thank you very much." She ignored reporters calling her name and disappeared into the building with her entourage.

Deepak Misra, on the other hand, did not speak to the media and waved away the microphones with dismissive gestures as he was led into the building by his attorney. The two families faced off in the courtroom. The Sharmas sat on the left-hand side and the faction of the Misra family who'd come to Cape Town, on the right.

The families of the three co-accused made quite a spectacle of themselves outside, yelling and shouting at each other and were banned from the proceedings.

The courtroom was now so quiet that one could have heard a pin drop.

Thutso Ndima, the driver, was called as the first witness of the prosecution. He testified that the attempted murder suspect, Deepak Misra, had boasted about organising another contract killing in South Africa before asking him to find him hitmen.

"Mr. Misra asked me as he booked the trip to Cape Point. I said NO, at first, but he offered me money that I couldn't reject. He told me that he had organised the murder of a friend's wife in PE three years ago and that it went down without a hitch. Wives are only trouble. That's what he said."

The Xhosa interpreter gave a little cough.

"Can you tell us anything else about this alleged hit in PE?" The prosecutor asked.

"He said that the tsotsi was not from South Africa

but from the UK and that he had come with Mr. Misra. But that it would work just as well with hitmen from Cape Town to make it look like a hijacking."

"Mr. Ndima, why do you think Mr. Misra would tell you a thing like that? About another crime he was allegedly involved in? Why would he do that?"

The driver thought for a moment. "I think he wanted to show me that he knows what he's doing. I told him that I have no experience with that, but he said money can solve any problem…"

"Did he, now?"

"Yes, sir. He said money solved problems before and how much do I want for helping kill the two women and his wife."

"Did he use these exact words?"

"Something like that, yes."

"Are you saying that Mr. Misra tried to recruit you to help him kill the two private investigators and his wife?"

"Yes. The two women he saw outside the hotel and maybe his wife. He wanted me and two other men. I asked in the township, in Gugulethu, if anybody knows tsotsis and I found Thami and Joe. When the hit went wrong, he changed his mind and wanted us to shoot his wife.

He paid 50% upfront in the morning before we went to Cape Point. He wanted to pay 50% back at the hotel."

"That is very detailed. Let it be known for the record, the accused is referring to his co-accused Thami Khetswayo and Joe Skenjana," the prosecutor said and the stenographer typed away. "Exhibit 2. A security tape from the hotel where Mr. Misra was staying, showing the handing-over of money to the co-accused." The prosecutor stepped forward and presented the evidence.

"How much did Mr. Misra pay you, and when and where?" He probed.

"He paid me 10,000 Rand in cash in a big envelope as a deposit. I ask for 15 but he said it's too much. Half of the money for me and half of the money split for Joe and Thami. He wanted to pay 25,000 when everything was done and his wife was dead. That's what he wanted to do."

"So Mr. Misra paid you the amount in cash? The deposit, as you call it."

"Yes, sir."

"And where did Mr. Misra give you that envelope

and when was that?"

"In the corner by the reception, where the toilets are, sir. And he gave me the envelope in the evening."

"Which evening?"

"The day before we went to Cape Point. I called him at six to say, yes, I found two men to help with the women. He was happy and said he is going out with his wife. I must wait in the lobby. He came later and gave me the deposit and we went out. I drove him to town."

"To town? You mean you took him to the Chinese Takeaway, where the shooting took place?"

"Yes," the interpreter said. "And then, Long Street."

"The brothel?"

"I don't know."

Deepak Misra's attorney kept looking at the witness, shaking his head.

"For the record, Mr. Ndima and two of his co-accused were convicted of firing a gun at two private detectives in front of a Chinese Take-Away shop in Greenpoint. This took place on the night before the staged hijacking and attempted murder Mr. Misra is on trial for. The three men were also convicted of attempted robbery the next day."

A loud murmur arose in the courtroom. Most people in the audience had missed that little detail.

"Objection, My Lord! Mr. Misra is not on trial for this incident," the star-attorney shouted into the quiet court-room."

"Sit down, Mr. Mandelbaum. Nobody implied that your client was on trial for this," the judge said wearily and paged through the documents before him. "So recorded."

"Where did you take Mr. Misra after that?" The prosecutor asked. "After the shooting in Greenpoint, the day before the attempted murder?"

"I took him to The Den in Long Street."

"Was this the first time, you'd taken him?"

"No, he sometimes wanted to go there after hours."

"Please explain to the court what kind of place The Den is."

The suspect continued to tell the court about the massage parlour and that Mr. Misra usually stayed for about one hour before going back to the hotel.

The defence lawyer was up next to cross-examine Thutso Ndima but despite his best efforts, he was unable to punch holes in the driver's testimony. He tried his best for the better part of one hour before the judge called for a recess. The cameras trained on Maribel recorded her expression of disgust.

In the days to come, the court would also hear evidence from the hired hitmen and that they were supposed to receive 5,000 Rand each from Deepak Misra.

Thami Khetswayo had counted the money on the morning of the attempted murder of Mr. Misra's wife. He was the so-called 'cousin'. Thereafter, the accounts of the co-accused diverted greatly from each other.

The part where Deepak Misra had visited the massage parlour was ruled as inadmissible due to the fact that, as his defence lawyer argued, it did not prove that he had been unfaithful to his new wife. "He could have conducted business there or received a massage for his neck problem. The driver never actually saw him enter or could say what Mr. Misra was planning to do there."

An angry murmur arose and the judge had to repeatedly ask for silence. The murmur died down when he threatened to have the courtroom cleared.

The entire time, the two sleuths sat at the back

behind the Sharma family and watched the proceedings unfold. The earrings Maribel was wearing distracted Charlie.

They were the same chandelier earrings she had seen in her dream! In the hotel van on that fateful day, the young bride had worn diamond studs. It baffled Charlie how some details of her nightmare had changed in real life. The most important change was, of course, that the murder attempt had not been successful.

Lerato was distracted by the thought of her client, who had still not responded to her e-mails. She could see her in the front with her niece, so the feisty PI decided to ask the aunt directly at the end of the first court day.

At last, the moment arrived.

"Thank you again for saving my life," Maribel said and hugged both Charlie and Lerato. "I made a mistake in marrying Deepak but at least it was not a fatal mistake." She was wearing a pale summer suit in contrast to the two older women in their colourful saris. She had told them about the two PIs.

"May I introduce you to my associate Charlie Proudfoot?" Lerato said. "She was with me all the way."

"It is so nice to meet you. So sorry this shameless man tried to kill you," Maribel's mother said. The two older women hugged Charlie and Lerato. "Thank you so much for preventing the worst. I am ever so grateful to you!"

"It all started with you, Mrs. Sharma," Lerato Gwala addressed the aunt. "If it hadn't been for you, your niece would have left this country in a coffin."

Mrs. Sharma looked confused. "What are you talking about, young lady? What did I do to prevent my niece's murder?"

Lerato stared at her wide-eyed. "Well, you contacted me three months ago and paid my expenses to work for you…"

"I did nothing of the sort, Ms Gwala! I had never even met Deepak until the wedding. My niece always went to England to visit him. We were introduced for the first time at their wedding in Chennai. I could feel that something was not quite right with this young man, but I certainly didn't know about his intentions."

"Then you didn't send me the e-mails that proved what he was planning to do?" Lerato asked. "You were not in England when you first called me?"

"No, ma chère, I did not send you any e-mails and I went to England only for the civil marriage before the honeymoon." The matron looked truly baffled.

"Well, I never! Lerato cried. "I didn't get a good look at you during that Skype call, because it was rather dark in the room. But didn't you say you were concerned about your niece's welfare?"

Aadiya Sharma put her hand on Lerato's arm. "Young lady, I certainly never Skype-called you and I am always concerned about my family's welfare, but if it was not I, then who could have known that Deepak Misra was planning to do our poor Maribel harm?" The two older women waggled their heads.

Lerato was flabbergasted. She was glad she hadn't mentioned the explicit images and e-mails she had received. This aunt would have fainted with shock.

In one of the photographs, Deepak's father had been in the background, observing his son and a man called David Cruikshank.

Where had these pictures and the e-mails come from? If this elderly woman in front of her had not called and paid her upfront for her services, then who had?

*

The Prafula Dubey murder investigations were threatening to go cold when the British police found several documents that pointed to Deepak Misra's involvement in her daughter Sarah's death three years ago in South Africa. They were mostly copies of emails and personal notes that turned out to be identical to the evidence in South Africa.

They proved that Sarah's husband, Robert Peele, had cooked up a plan to kill her beloved daughter with Deepak's help.

They also proved that Sarah was sick and tired of her husband's many affairs and disrespect for her. Prafula had recommended that Sarah should see a divorce lawyer. He must have found out somehow and asked Deepak Misra to organise an assassin.

A surgeon by the name of David was mentioned several times. Nobody had found out about their plot and Sarah's murder had been declared an accidental death.

How Prafula Dubey had gotten hold of their correspondence was unclear, but she had taken her revenge during their clandestine sessions in the cheap hotel in London, where she could do as she pleased, while her husband did as he pleased.

She could not be sure whether Deepak had known that Sarah was her daughter. He was so shallow that he didn't even care to ask about her children.

As a teenager, Sarah had moved to South Africa to attend boarding school in Port Elizabeth. When she had refused to marry the man her old-fashioned father had chosen for her, Sarah was turned into a virtual outcast.

Prafula had remained in touch with her daughter, although her husband did not permit her attendance of the white wedding. She had shed tears in solitude and acted out her anger with men, who were so inclined.

Most of them yearned to be humiliated and Prafula had been more than willing to comply with their wishes.

Officially, she attended an all-female yoga class in London and that excuse had never been questioned by her husband. Although she did visit a gym regularly and had been seen there, nobody in her yoga class had ever come close to the quarter where she was meeting her customers.

When news of Sarah's murder broke, Vikesh, her husband had commented that she had it coming and nobody should be surprised. Least of all her own mother.

That heartless prick! Her anger was ready to erupt.

When Deepak had told her about the imminent wedding to a pretty and educated young Indian woman, she couldn't contain her hatred any longer. He confided in her that if his new wife did not comply with his wishes, he would kill her as well.

Her revenge had been simple enough and Prafula had followed the actions of the private investigators with great satisfaction.

Lerato Gwala was the only female detective, she had been able to find online. She did for Deepak's bride what she could not do for her own daughter. Money was no object.

But not everything went as planned.

On the last day of her unhappy life, Prafula had noticed that someone was following her as she left the gym in High Street late that afternoon. Nonsense, she told herself, who would be following me anywhere? She had waved her friends goodbye after their yoga class and walked towards her Jaguar at the far end of the parking lot. She never suspected that a hired killer was following her in the dark.

Before she could reach the Jaguar, he'd swooped

in and forced her into a waiting car. They had tortured her in a secluded spot in the forest and extracted the information they wanted.

About her relationship with Deepak, the e-mails she had stolen. Everything. She had begged them to let her go but the men had just laughed in her face. "Maybe you shouldn't make important enemies," the thickset brown-haired man had told her. He'd done most of the beating.

It could only mean that Ashwin must have found out. She offered them more money than what he was paying them.

"Do you think we're stupid?" the one with the straggly blond hair sneered.

"You will go straight to the police. Then we'll be up shit's creek. I'd rather that you're in trouble, old lady."

They had laughed and given her a few more slaps, then taken her to a boat and tied her feet together. She pleaded with them until they grew tired of her yammering and put duct tape over her mouth. The men tied heavy rocks around her waist and dropped her overboard.

The police arrested Ashwin Misra at his office in

front of shocked staff members. They had never particularly liked his harsh nature and that he was working them to the bone, but never in their wildest dreams had they expected the police to arrest their boss. They learned that the arrest had something to do with the Berkshire Murder.

Witnesses had come forward and told the detectives that they had gone for a hike and what they had seen in the forest a week before the woman was found floating in the river. Their statement convinced the police. The timeline matched and they knew that they weren't dealing with one of those futile leads that sent them on a wild goose chase.

"We've seen couples, who come to the forest to have a bit of fun. That's why we assumed that somebody was playing out 50 Shades. It was a bit much, so we just went off in the other direction," one of the hikers said when questioned why they had not come forward sooner. "People are weird and we sometimes see strange stuff."

The penny dropped when details of the killing appeared in the local newspaper. The hikers had passed a black car on the path and one of them could unbelievably remember the last four numbers on the license plate, and that it was a Toyota.

It hadn't taken the police long to find the owner of the car. A man with straggly blond hair opened his door to loud knocking by the police. When interrogated, it turned out that he was an acquaintance of David Cruikshank, the man who'd accompanied Deepak Misra to South Africa three years earlier. The man who had been killed in a police shootout.

At first, the man denied any wrong-doing, then he implicated his brother-in-law who had talked him into doing a job for a rich businessman from Reading. No, he had never met the toff before and didn't know his name – but his brother-in-law did.

Ashwin Misra and the two hapless henchmen were charged with kidnapping, conspiracy to murder, murder and attempt to defeat the ends of justice.

TV viewers were spellbound by the two intertwined cases and news reporters began to camp outside the courthouse in Cape Town, to catch every episode of this real-life soap opera.

Maribel Misra, who now called herself Maribel Sharma, was the last witness on the stand. "I will never forget it. Deepak Misra said, 'shit, shit, shit' and 'hurry up, you morons!'"

"In those exact words?" The prosecutor turned to the audience and then faced the witness again.

"Yes, pretty much," Maribel answered.

"And what did the other men present at the time of the incident say?"

"The driver said, 'we cannot do that, sir. The police are coming.'" Maribel looked calmly at the audience.

"And what did Mr. Misra do or say then?"

"I remember it clearly. He said, 'give me the iron! I'll do it myself!' Then the police came and arrested all of them."

Despite the mounting evidence, the judge had different ideas of what constituted evidence and wouldn't allow a witness from England, a former lover of the accused, to testify. He was of the opinion that this was not directly related to the case at hand.

Against expectations, Deepak Misra was cleared of all charges and incredulous viewers watched his grinning face on their television sets and cell phones. The prosecution had allegedly not proved their case beyond reasonable doubt and he walked out of the courtroom a free man.

Pandemonium reigned inside and outside the court, and social media very nearly collapsed under the flood of posts. But all was not lost.

As soon as the star attorney and his grinning client were leaving the Cape High Court, they were served with a folded document. It was a summons in connection with another murder three years before in Port Elizabeth.

Reading the document wiped his grin right off the attorney's face. Deepak was handcuffed in front of wildly clicking cameras and taken into custody. No more privileges of staying at a five-star hotel or seeing a psychologist of his choice. Now it was the Sharma-family's turn to rejoice.

Although Deepak Misra had not been found guilty of his wife's attempted murder, he had been arrested on suspicion of having orchestrated the murder of Sarah Peele, the wife of his late friend and business partner in Port Elizabeth.

This was too good to be true! News headlines were printed and pictures of the very public arrest flashed across TV screens.

During the evening news, the Misra spokesman gave an interview at a large South African television station.

"Can you enlighten our viewers with regards to the new situation? Your client has been re-arrested. Did this come as a shock to you?" The presenter asked the visibly agitated man.

"Of course it came as a shock. In our opinion, the South African police are conducting a politically-motivated smear campaign against my client to protect their tourism industry. This new case is a total fabrication. Just as we feared, this is a tragic miscarriage of justice in a developing country with a corrupt justice system. My client is the victim here."

"But Mr. Misra was just acquitted by a South African High Court of all charges against him. Would you consider this also a miscarriage of justice?"

"No, of course not. In this outcome, we cannot fault the South African courts but he should never have been accused of this crime in the first place. Extradited to be made a scapegoat! It just shows how unfairly my client was treated."

"But you can't have it both ways. If your client is indeed the victim of malicious prosecution, then how do you explain this acquittal? Was it unfair to find him not guilty? And isn't it true that your client was not subjected to incarceration during his trial but was accommodated in every way according to his attorney's requests?"

"Mr. Misra should not have been extradited in the first place! It is clear that he will not receive a fair trial until this country sees him in prison. The National Police Commissioner called him a monkey. I beg your pardon… a monkey?!"

"I see. The Police Commissioner is known for making shocking remarks. Can you give us any insight into new revelations why the father of the accused, Mr. Ashwin Misra, was recently arrested in England on charges of murder related to the recent death of a Prafula Dubey? Isn't this the reason why he could not be present in Cape Town at his son's trial?"

The spokesman lost his cool. He unclipped the microphone from his lapel and stormed huffing and puffing out of the studio. The camera crane followed his every move until the enraged man was out of sight.

"We would like to apologise to our viewers," the presenter said and listened to instructions in her earpiece.

"And will now show you excerpts of this case."

The police investigations in Britain soon revealed that Ashwin Misra had Prafula Dubey killed to protect his son. She had been his long-time lover, and there was no doubt in his mind who was behind the e-mail evidence presented during the trial in Cape Town.

The wealthy businessman had hired a thug called Rafe Wilson to break into the woman's car. That's how a laptop with e-mails and compromising pictures was discovered, and that she had forwarded the evidence to the Maitirelo Private Detective Agency in Johannesburg. He'd abducted Prafula Dubey with the help of his brother-in-law and the two thugs had killed her.

It was sheer luck that Prafula's body had resurfaced before the whole affair had blown over and the connection to the Misra case could be made. It was the first time Ashwin Misra's damage control had failed, and for the first time, he would face the music himself.

The public was almost disappointed that the Berkshire case had been solved, but there was yet another trial in South Africa that one could look forward to.

*

Jono Morake poured boiling water over tea bags in two cups. He added milk and handed Charlie her vanilla tea before taking a sip from his cup. He liked his tea with milk and two spoons of sugar. The way his sister liked it before she had developed a problem with sugar.

"Back to tea, I see," Charlie said with a twinkle in her eye. As so often, Charlie twisted the wedding ring she was still wearing. Colin's name and their wedding date were engraved inside.

"Mhmm."

"So, what's news with you?" Charlie asked her brother. The two dogs had settled on the carpet and watched their every move.

"Turns out, it's simply not enough to know your hardware. Rowena was emotionally totally immature, and into boozing like you won't believe. No matter where we went, she always knew some people at the joint and wanted to do shots with them. And here I was, the outsider, bored out of his skull."

"Sorry to hear that, Jono. I thought she was quite attractive."

"Definitely. The other guys clearly thought so, too."

"So, did the two of you split up?"

"You already know?" Jono seemed surprised.

"Well, it doesn't take a mind reader to figure that one out."

"Yes, we split up. It wasn't what you could call a relationship, anyway. So there. Just two weeks of mind-boggling sex."

"Eeyew, I didn't need to know that!" Charlie cried.

Jono shrugged his shoulders and chortled.

"On a different note, I brought a little something for you from Cape Town."

"A little something? What with all that excitement and near-fatal encounters with criminals, you still found the time to go shopping? Somebody help me understand women," he said, looking at the ceiling.

"Not shopping, as such," Charlie said and Jono gave her a disbelieving stare.

"Okay, Woolies had a sale on and we picked up some bargains."

"Gee, thanks a lot. So I'm getting a bargain?"

"Don't be ungrateful, big brother, or I'm going to wear it myself."

"Okay, you have my attention."

Charlie pulled out a long fluffy, blue garment from a Woolies plastic bag.

"What on earth is that supposed to be?"

"A onesie."

He took turns staring at his sister and at the long polar fleece thing she was holding up. "What's a onesie?"

"Jono! This is for winter, of course. You wear it as pyjamas when it's cold. And it has a hood, too, see. I can take off the ears if you don't like them." The hood was effectively the face of a teddy bear with ears on each side.

"You're kidding, right? No ways am I going to wear something that looks like a baby-grow. Like ever!" He pushed his hand through his unruly hair.

"Nobody will see it, but it's so warm and comfy. I got myself a onesie, too… and Lerato bought herself the same in a panda bear look."

"You've lost your mind, sis. And it's slam-bam in the middle of summer, by the way. It's way too hot to wear something like that."

"I know, silly. That's why it was on special. Come

another freezing winter in Joburg, you will thank me for it. I also got one and so did Lerato. In different colours."

Charlie took out another fluffy, light-coloured garment with a unicorn on top of the hood. "See?" She beamed at him persuasively.

"You think I'll eat my words? We'll see about that. But thank you for sparing a thought for your older brother in the middle of a murder case, Madam Detective."

"I'm not a detective and have no intention of ever becoming one. I want to live my life in peace and quiet."

"Whatever you say, Charlie. Where is Lerato? Recuperating from your ordeal?"

"She stayed in Cape Town for another week. Visiting friends and family."

The phone shrilled in the living room. "Damn, I wanted to phone Mom in New York today and totally forgot about it," Charlie said as they walked to the living room.

"How do you know it's Mom?" Jono asked.

"I don't know, I'm just guessing."

"Right." Jono grinned. How often had he heard that one before?

"Are you coming or what?" Charlie asked him and

raced him to the living room. Jono picked up the receiver.

"Hi, Mom. Yes, she is. Wait, I'll put you on speakerphone."

Motshabi Morake's voice was as smooth as velvet and full of warmth as she spoke to the eldest of her brood. "That would be good. Then I can speak to both of you at the same time."

"Hi there, Mom!" Charlie called over Jono's shoulder.

"Hi, my darling!" Motshabi Morake greeted her cheerfully. "So what have you kids been up to?"

The End

THE AUTHOR

Evadeen Brickwood grew up with two sisters in Germany and studied cultural sciences and languages. As a young woman, she travelled extensively and many of her books are inspired by her experiences abroad. Feeling adventurous, the newly qualified translator moved to Africa in 1988 and worked for two years as a secretary and language teacher in Botswana. The author eventually settled in South Africa, where she got married and raised two daughters.

In Johannesburg, Evadeen Brickwood studied computers and management of training and worked as a corporate software trainer, professional translator and lecturer at WITS University. In 2003, she began her writing career with youth novels in the 'Remember the Future' series, about adventures in prehistory. Book 1, the award-winning 'Children of the Moon', has been published twice in South Africa and translated into German. The author now self-publishes and you can look forward to the new, off-beat Charlie Proudfoot series, which is set in South Africa.

The author's websites are:

http://www.evadeen.wixsite.com/charlieproudfoot

http://www.evadeen.wixsite.com/novels

http://www.evadeen.wixsite.com/youngbooks

Evadeen is looking forward to your mail and can also be contacted on social media, incl. Facebook, Twitter, Instagram, Pinterest, google+ and Goodreads.

ABOUT THIS EPISODE

I've been carrying around the idea of writing a slightly paranormal murder mystery series for a while, and since I've been living in South Africa for many years, it made sense to set the stories in this alluring country. I had the name of the series and that I wanted a paranormal aspect, but like so many of us, I was bogged down by a busy lifestyle. Then the pandemic hit and everything came to a grinding halt. For the first month or so, I tried to adapt to the strict lockdown. I pondered, how life would continue, painted landscapes on my garden walls, sewed summer dresses and watched YouTube videos. Then I remembered the book project that I'd had at the back of my mind for so long and began writing. The lockdown in 2020 produced the initial three books in the series and I'm planning to publish at least 2 episodes per year. This pilot episode was inspired by the Anni Dewani murder case, that left us all with a bitter taste in the mouth, after the main suspect, her new husband, was released after a drawn-out legal battle. What went wrong? We'll never know, but I wrote an entirely new storyline and hope you enjoy the read and the South African flavour. The second episode has an entirely different theme: wildlife conservation and you won't have to wait long to find out who murdered our victim in this story.

THE NEXT EPISODE
in the Charlie Proudfoot Series

2

When Professor Gerald Morton does not return
from observing a pack of endangered
African wild dogs in the Kruger Park,
his project team makes
a gruesome discovery in the bush.
Is somebody trying to sabotage their research?
And what does the professor's ex-wife
have to do with his murder?

MORE BOOKS BY
EVADEEN BRICKWOOD

This adventure mystery tells the story of 22-year-old Bridget Reinhold who is not exactly the adventurous type, but when her sister Claire disappears in Southern Africa, nothing can hold her in England. Bridget launches herself into the search in Botswana and encounters obstacle after obstacle. She learns the basics of the native language and culture and soon moves to the capital city of Gaborone. Soon, her mission is plunged into turmoil as everything seems to be going wrong. Just coincidence or is there something more sinister at work?

Another mystery novel set in modern South Africa. This time, the murders of a ranger and a rare black rhino in the idyllic Shangari Safari Park rattle the local community of Rutgersdrift. Sofia Helenius from Finland lives at the lodge with her boyfriend Tom Rutgers, the owner of Shangari. Sofia is tormented by a secret she yearns to share with Tom, but the cruel events grab the limelight and put everything else in the shade. One of the native Khoi-San families is known to communicate with wild animals, but what if the criminals get wind of this gift?

When another murder happens in the city of Johannesburg, smouldering secrets begin to unravel. How are the murders connected and will it be possible to halt a relentless crime-syndicate in order to save an African paradise?

As if growing up in the seventies wasn't difficult enough, teenager Isabell Bertrand is also too rebellious for her parents' liking. A novel treatment with hypnosis appears to be the perfect remedy and Dr. Albrecht regresses Isabell to her early childhood and even further back. She experiences previous lifetimes and then one in particular: could this beautiful young woman in a silk sari, who was forced to choose between two men, really once have been her? Years later, Isabell is invited to a wedding in Pakistan and memories of a forgotten love come flooding back - with dangerous consequences.

Can you imagine, suddenly living in the past? Not last year or in the Roman Empire, but a really, really long time ago?

Katherine, Trevor and Chryséis embark on a sea voyage and sail across the prehistoric ocean to the remnants of a sunken continent. Suddenly everybody seems to be after a mysterious speaking stone from the fabled land of Lyonesse.

Finding their way back to Alesia and their home in the future, turns out to be more difficult than the time travellers thought. War breaks out in the Mediterranean Sea and forces Katherine, Trevor and Chryséis to flee inland. Nothing here is the way they thought it would be, and who has ever heard of Egypt without pyramids?